The Art of Worship

A NOVELLA

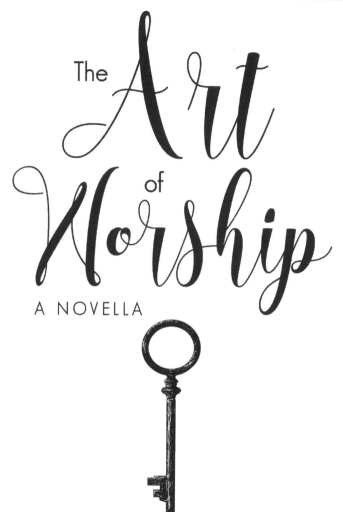

KILBY BLADES

Published by Luxe Press 2017

For permission requests and other inquiries, the publisher can be reached at: info@luxepress.net.

ISBN-13: 978-0-9991532-0-8
ISBN-10: 0-9991532-0-X

Editor: Plot Bunny Editing, www.plotbunnyediting.com

Cover Design: Elizabeth Mackey, www.elizabethmackeygraphics.com

Custom Formatting: Champagne Formats,
www.champagneformats.com

PA Services: Britta Neal

Promotion Services: Jennifer Reynolds, www.jenniferrpromotions.com

Dedication

To Marcia

Chapter One

The Rules

Reed

"Reed, may I see you in my study?"

My father's casual tone is misplaced, as if he invites me into his study with regularity. Which he doesn't.

"I thought that since your mother was out, we might have a talk, just the two of us."

As we walk silently from the kitchen toward the eastern wing of the house, I wonder what this could be about. I'm eighteen, a senior in high school. My grades are excellent. I never stay out past curfew or get in trouble. And if he ever found the small stash of pot I keep in my underwear drawer, I doubt he'd care.

But there are some things Preston Whitney takes seriously—like anything that happens in his study. And I'm curious to know why he's summoned me. It's a distinguished space. The handcrafted wood shelves that stand from floor to ceiling hold first editions of classics and other rare books. The furniture has been passed down through generations, along with mementos from across the globe. A fire blazes brightly in a hearth nearly as tall as the two of us. An old phonograph playing Chopin crackles and whines.

Every time I'm here, I get the feeling that I am stepping into another century. I half expect the portraits of Whitney men that hang on the walls to come alive. These men are more serious versions of my father—oceanic eyes stare down past haughty cheekbones. One day it will be my own son and great-grandson who stand in this room inspecting a portrait of me.

"Scotch?" he asks, closing the door needlessly before striding to his liquor trolley.

It places me on alert. He only likes us to drink together when he has something to get off his chest. The last time he called me in for a man-to-man was the night they gave me the Jeep. We'd gotten through a third of a bottle of Blue Label before he'd said his peace on the privilege of driving a car and the responsibilities that go along with it.

"Thank you," I accept, in a tone as cordial and controlled as his. For as much as I'm just a kid, I've been well-trained in the protocols of high-born men.

I take a seat on the leather chair that faces his direction just as he pulls out a well-aged Laphroaig. I study him, for clues, as he drops a single cube of ice into each tumbler, pours us each two fingers of whiskey, and travels to join me in the chair opposite mine. He gives away nothing and, as usual, I don't know whether to resent his cool composure or to respect the hell out of his discipline. No teenage kid wants to admit to idolizing his dad, but in many ways, I do.

He settles in next to me, resting the bottle on the table between us as he places one of the tumblers in my hand. I meet his eyes, and we raise our glasses in a silent toast, before turning our gazes to the fire. The whiskey tastes good and I make a mental note to raid his supply. The cheap stuff is fine for the flask I bring to school, but I wouldn't mind enjoying a nip or two of this in the privacy of my own room.

"You and Aubrey are close," he begins after a few minutes.

Hmmm…he wants to talk about Aubrey.

"Your mother seems to think you two are—*being intimate*—with each other."

Brilliant—now they're speculating on my sex life.

"Are you?"

I feel his eyes slide back to me. I keep my face neutral, my eyes on the crackling fire.

"Yes, we're very close," I say calmly.

"But have you been intimate with one another?"

To anyone else, his voice would have sounded perfectly

even, but I sense his slight annoyance. He doesn't like how good I've become at his subtle brand of insolence. The corner of my mouth quirks upwards in amusement as I look back over at him. I think about apples and trees and things that don't fall far from one another.

"Are you referring to the special way a man and a woman hug when they love one another?"

Yes, it's wicked of me, but he's asking for it. He's a doctor—can't he just come out and say "sex"?

"You underestimate me, Reed," he retorts evenly. "Even if you can't believe that I was your age once, at least give me credit for living closer to reality than the other parents in this town. Remember, I'm the one prescribing their kids birth control and helping them figure out what to do when they don't use it."

I want to tell him not to underestimate *me*, to give *me* credit for not being like the kids I go to school with but I think the better of it. I distill my thoughts into a more diplomatic response.

"Don't worry, Dad. I know that the pill is over 97% effective if taken as directed. I know that condoms and abstinence are the only ways to reduce the risk of STDs, and that condoms must be applied properly—with the tip pulled up flat and empty—in order for them to work."

See how I threw in that shit about abstinence? It never hurts to keep your parents guessing.

"I know you know those things. I know you'll take measures to protect you and Aubrey and I hope you know that if anything unexpected happens you can trust your mother and me enough to come to us for help."

And it's true. My parents are decent people, and I've got it better than a lot of kids. They'd be pissed if I got Aubrey pregnant, but they wouldn't freak out, and I respect them for that.

Conceding, I say "I appreciate that...but, Dad...why are we here?"

He swirls his glass again, the remaining sliver of ice a mere shard floating in honey-colored liquid. I follow suit as he looks back toward the hearth, patiently waiting for him to reveal the purpose of our conversation.

"Have I ever told you how much your grandmother Eleanor disapproved of your mother?"

I shake my head and straighten in my seat a little. He almost never speaks of his parents, who were killed in a small plane crash years before I was born. I am surprised, and intrigued, that he speaks of them now and that any of it has to do with my mother. For years, I've been eager to know more about them.

"She wouldn't even give me her engagement ring to ask for your mother's hand. Even though Kate came from her own money, she came up with every excuse for why we shouldn't be together. She thought Kate was after our money, that she was pursuing other men simultaneously for *their* money, that she was sleeping with other men...she named every conceivable charge you could level against a woman trying to marry into a family like ours."

"Why she believed this about your mother was a different story, a misunderstanding I'll share with you at another time. But your grandfather, my father, never believed a word of it. He knew not only that your mother loved me, but that she was loyal, and would be a faithful wife. He knew I never had to worry about her straying from me because our love was real."

He turns back to look at me pointedly.

"He knew I could satisfy her every need."

Wait…what?

He can't mean—

When my father raises a confirming eyebrow, I can only gape in mortification.

Jesus, dad—TMI!

As he lets his subtext fully sink in, I flush with embarrassment.

"Son, you are here to receive a precious gift. It is one that my father bestowed upon me, and that his father bestowed upon him—one I will pass on to you now and expect that you give to your own sons when it is time."

What. The. Fuck?

"You are a Whitney, and were therefore born with certain natural—*endowments*—that predispose you to success with women. But, there is a beauty in sex which, if you could only grow to appreciate it—an art which, if you could only commit to learning it—will bring you and the women in your life such divine fulfillment as most mortals never know. It is the art of worship, Reed, and it has very little to do with sex."

His gaze is intense and I can barely breathe, let alone process my surprise that such a cache of Whitney family wisdom exists. My father is subtle most of the time, but when he isn't he can be intimidating. It doesn't help that he's hit the nail on the head about my need for some, erm…guidance. The truth is, I've been worried about pleasing Aubrey.

"So, I'll ask you again, son. Have you and Aubrey been intimate with one another?"

I shake my head in sheepish truth.

"But, you plan to be."

I nod.

"Very good…" he smiles, polishing off the rest of his glass, "…then, there's still time."

I stare dumbly at the fire, suspended in anticipation as my father refills our glasses. He takes his time retrieving more ice, pouring more whiskey, and returning to his seat. When he pushes the glass into my hand, his eyes drill into mine.

"The first, and most important, rule is that Whitney men don't fuck. We never give over to the monster. That doesn't mean sex can't be vigorous—only that we must maintain a modicum of control. We surrender only to our devotion for the woman before us."

I nod my understanding.

"I won't lie—it'll be difficult at your age. Your hormones

will entice you to think only about yourself without regard for your partner."

I straighten in my chair. "I am completely devoted to Aubrey." One day, sooner than anyone thinks, I'm going to ask that girl to marry me. My father nods his approval.

"Good. Then, you're ready for the second rule: always take care of her first—and don't be lazy about it. Bring her all the pleasure she can stand, as slowly as she can take it, before you go seeking yours."

The advice makes enough sense so far, and this is less tense than I had feared. But I can't bring myself to ask for specifics.

"What if she makes it—" I stumble. Better to start with an easier question.

...hard?

"—difficult? What if I try to satisfy her, but she wants to...move it along?"

His eyes register understanding. "With time, you'll build enough stamina to please her first, even if you skip right to it. Until then, persuade her to let you slow things down, to show her the joys of foreplay."

Foreplay has been an elusive concept. I barely understand the what, and I'm lost on the how long. But my father isn't finished, so I say nothing.

"You'll need to become as adept at calming her as you are at exciting her. Particularly if she's inexperienced, you will want her as relaxed as possible. Having you inside her will be painful."

I nod and bury my nose in my tumbler, taking a long sip of my drink. I have questions, and I wish I could be as uninhibited with him as he's being with me. But the two of us talking like this is still too surreal.

"What's rule number three?"

"That every woman is different and only she can teach you what she likes. So, forget everything you've seen in porno movies and whatever lies the other boys tell in the locker room. When you're with Aubrey, listen for the words she says and the clues her body gives you—does her breathing change when you kiss her this place or that? Does she pull your body towards certain parts of hers? And don't just listen for what she's encouraging you to do—read the signs when she's telling you what not to do, as well. For example, if she's vocal with appreciation for one thing, she may be quiet when you do something she dislikes. Does she push towards you when she wants more of something? If so, she may pull away from you if she wants less of something. It is hard work, at the beginning, to read a woman's signs. But her body is talking to you—it's telling you what to do."

I contemplate my time with Aubrey and know I haven't been as thorough as he is suggesting. I always felt that some part of her wanted more from me, and it wasn't just about going all the way. Her kisses (fuck, so delicious) are hungry and I can feel she's craving something, but I've barely known for what.

"Do you have questions, son?"

What if I can't read the signs? What if she's too

inexperienced to even know what she wants, much less indicate it? What if I'm too inexperienced to understand or give it to her? And, damnit, dad, why are you holding out on me? Where is all the Whitney wisdom on how to touch a woman's g-spot and her clit and even her nipples in ways that drive her wild? Surely, grandfather gave you at least that…

"No," I say shaking my head.

He rises, and I take it as my cue to do the same.

"Then we'll continue our conversation next week."

Next week?

He slaps his hand on my shoulder as he leads us out of his study. When we reach the back stairs, he's smiling broadly and his eyes are playful, and proud.

"In the meantime, son…*practice.*"

Chapter Two

Practice

Aubrey

On Friday nights, my dad always works, and Reed comes over to "do homework". *Homework*, of course, culminates in us making out in my bedroom, and we've created a simple ruse to guarantee our privacy. Reed bought a few of those prepaid cell phones they sell in Middletown. We always know where the underage parties will be, so we've gotten in the habit of disguising our voices and calling in anonymous complaints whenever someone we don't like is having one. Bernice, the sixty-three-year-old biddy on the night switchboards has hearing so bad, she's never recognized us. I doubt she ever would, even if we used our real voices.

It's now 10:00. Actual homework has been done. In case my dad shows up by surprise, books lie open and pencils are strewn strategically across the dining room table. The call has been placed. The police scanner feed on my father's too-easy-to-hack computer confirms that he has been dispatched. And I'm not-so-subtly dragging Reed to my room.

Between his baseball practices and my history project, not to mention piles of regular homework, we've hardly seen each other all week. I am ravenous for him, and the way my lips assault his before the door even closes behind us lets him know as much.

He responds immediately, his tongue snaking in eagerly to stroke mine, his kiss thorough and deep. I drown in it blissfully until he releases my mouth for air. I moan as he drags his nose down my neck, as he pulls the flat collar of my shirt aside to bite down on my shoulder. I whimper in helpless pleasure. I can't help what he does to me.

"Goddamn, Aubrey..." he moans, pressing himself to my hip to let me feel how hard he is.

It's always like this between us—always dangerously incendiary—and fuck, if Reed Whitney doesn't make me want him. We've been together since we met Freshman year. We've each lived in the same town all our lives, but the two middle schools in the district feed into a single, much larger, high school. And the two of us are desperately in love.

I want everything with this man—my first time, moving

to the city, building a life together, and a family one day. It's that all-consuming want that makes me put the brakes on sometimes, but I'm all too eager tonight. When I've slowed us down in the past, I've let him think I have the common jitters, but I haven't been honest with him about my *other* fears.

I've gone through my life knowing I was the mistake of two teenagers who thought they were in love, but weren't. Their naiveté, of course, had dire consequences—a child who was never meant to be born, a marriage that made an honest woman out of my mother but a liar out of them both, a broken home that turned me into a pinball who bounced among parents, grandparents, and other far-flung relatives. I'm resolute that this brand of madness should begin, and end, with me.

Most of me accepts that this has no bearing on Reed and me. That we aren't Greg and Dierdre. That I will simultaneously use the pill, condoms, spermicidal gel, and a diaphragm every time I have sex until I finish graduate school if it means avoiding what my parents went through. Deep down, I know that if Reed and I made love right now, it would be beautiful and sweet and irrevocably right. Indeed, I've been letting up on the brakes in recent weeks, a fact that hasn't escaped his notice.

What surprises me now is how it is Reed who seems to be backpedaling. It's like something has him spooked. Maybe he's afraid that I'm unsure? I guess I'll just have to prove to him otherwise.

"Touch me, Reed." I beg, pressing my body right back into his.

"Tell me where, love."

Hmm…that's new.

Usually he lavishes me with touches on my whole body, letting his hands run up and down my arms, or caressing my face with fingertips before tucking back my hair. I dream of the moments when the backs of his fingers graze my breasts and his palm cups my dampened sex.

"*Everywhere,*" I whisper.

I squeak like a little mouse when he lifts me up before taking a short few steps and depositing me gently on the bed. There is something different in his eyes as he strips me down to my bra and panties—something different from the dozens of times he's done it before. By the time he wears only gray boxer briefs, I lay transfixed by the sight of his body, by the quarter-sized wet spot on the front of his skivvies. I arch my body up, hoping he'll blanket himself on top of me as he has so many times before, but he doesn't. He slides in on one side of me and props himself up on his elbow.

"Please, Aubrey…" he beseeches, his blue-green irises as hypnotic as pendula, "I want to know what drives you mad. Show me…"

I want to take his hand and slip it beneath my panties, to slide his long, glorious finger across my wetness as proof that he already knows that driving me crazy is exactly what he is doing. But something stops me. He's serious. I reach out to stroke his jaw, and when my fingers touch, he closes his eyes. His expression is somewhat pained, and for the first time, the most obvious of thoughts occurs to me.

Reed Whitney—this gorgeous, magic-tongued god who has more sex in his pinkie finger than most teenage boys have in their whole bodies—is nervous. As if I didn't already combust in his presence. As if he didn't have my lady parts begging for more. With compassion for his unlikely humanity, I throw him a bone.

"I like it when you bite my shoulder…"

He bows his head and gives me a gentle nip. I reach for his hand and bring it up to my hardened nipple, so he can see the effect he's having, and bite my lip to stifle a smile when I hear his soft moan. He's being so cute, I decide to throw him another.

"…and when you run your fingers down my legs…"

God, I love watching those long fingers touch me. His pressure is light, a soft caress. He seems transfixed by the goose bumps he has caused to pebble my skin. He's backed himself into a kneeling position at the foot of the bed, and slowly lifts my heel to his shoulder. Turning his head, he begins kissing up my calf. It is heavenly, and even through my pleasure, I think of that thing he stumbled upon once—the thing I'd been *dying* for him to do again.

"Fuck…and when you lick my ankles."

He raises an eyebrow in surprised interest, and had his fulfillment of my request not caused me to lose the power of coherent speech, I may have shot back a snarky retort. All conversation stops when instinct takes over and doesn't resume until we curse simultaneously at the sound of his phone alarm.

"Fifteen minutes 'till curfew," he says needlessly, the regret in his voice evident.

Regret, indeed. It was our hottest make out session yet.

"Maybe we can pick this up tomorrow? At the duck pond?" I suggest hopefully.

A brilliant grin lights his face before he bends down to kiss me.

"Maybe…"

And he leaves me a minute later. I don't even wait for the sound of the front door to slam before I slide my fingers in my panties to finish what he started.

Reed

I race up the stairs the second I get home, my leaking cock begging me for something—anything—to relieve the pressure. I barely make it to the shower before I start stroking myself, reliving the sounds of moans I'd never heard from her as I worked her, over and over, with simple things I'd never known she loved. When I remember the soft "yes" she hissed when I licked her ankle, I lose it, panting quietly as my essence gushes over my fist. After a slow, lazy lather with only my Axe shower gel and more memories that won't stop flooding my mind, I realize I'm hard again. After my second go, it takes me a solid twenty minutes to catch my breath and pull myself together.

With pruny fingers and a dopey grin I can't seem to wipe off of my face, I put on pajamas and head down the back stairs. This is all under the auspices of going to the kitchen to make myself a sandwich. Secretly, I'm hoping that my father is in his study, that he will remember his promise to talk again soon and invite me in, even though it hasn't yet been a week.

My mom is still visiting colleges with my twin sister, Nikki, and I've noticed how restless my dad has been. Especially when my mother is away, he has night owl tendencies—I know he has to be awake.

I take my time assembling my ham and cheese sandwich, grilling it lightly in butter as I contemplate my approach.

"Smells good."

His voice breaks me out of my reverie, and I smile in the direction of the skillet before turning to face him.

"Want one?"

"Thank you," he says, with a nod.

We make smalltalk, about how Nikki likes each of the campuses she's visited, about how helpless and malnourished we are without mom's cooking, about the hijinks of the townspeople that week at the hospital. After we finish our sandwiches and put the dishes in the dishwasher, we stand facing each other.

Here goes.

"So I practiced."

"And?"

"You were right. She was giving me clues—when I paid better attention, she really seemed to, uh…" I scratched my head, "…respond."

He smiles as tactfully as possible, but I can see the pride.

"What did it teach you?"

I think about it.

"Well, the things she liked…were kind of obscure. I expected her to want me to touch her a certain way, you know, in all the obvious places…but the things she liked best were really little things, on parts of her body that were nowhere near…"

I cut myself off, and he doesn't make me finish.

"Good…you're learning."

I don't know what to say next. He looks thoughtful, but otherwise unreadable, so I get set to make my retreat.

"Do you have time for scotch, son? Maybe we could continue our conversation. That is, if you're not too tired."

I shake my head and bite back a smile.

"No, I'm not too tired."

He pours the first drink, and as I wait, I find that, this time around, I am more aware of the paintings of my forefathers. I'd always fancied them to be gruff old men, as rigid and formal as their portrait poses. But now I wonder: who had they really been? Had they loved their wives, as my father loves my mother, or had they 'worshipped' many women?

Handing me my glass, my dad takes his seat and drills

me with that serious look again, the one that tells me he's about to say something important.

"Tonight we'll talk anatomy, and we'll start with a woman's most important sexual organ: *her mind.*"

He'd been so right the first time that I abandon my usual snark. This time, I'm hanging on his every word. I wouldn't mind taking notes, and the more I think about it, I consider that maybe I ought to write this down when I get back to my room. I suddenly take this responsibility very seriously and I imagine that, one day, I'll have sons of my own.

"Nothing will compensate for failing to get her in the right mental state—not years of experience, not flawless technique, not even a huge Whitney cock."

Yeah, he's talking about us.

"Think, Reed. Two people don't just find themselves in the bedroom—something gets them there. Something that may not be sexual at all sparks a sexual attraction. Now, you have to figure out what things do that for Aubrey. Does she get off on the way you look at her? The words you say to her and how you say them? Does she like the way you smell? To this day, I can't eat an ice cream cone in front of your mother without—"

Jesus, Dad—keep it clean!

"Can we please focus on Aubrey?"

He at least has the decency to look sheepish.

"Tell me…when, outside of your time in the bedroom, does Aubrey seem particularly affected by you?"

I'm usually pretty good at sensing when girls are dazzled

by me, but Aubrey is harder to read. I think back hard, to things I've noticed, but everything I come up with seems pretty innocuous to me.

"She blushes when I fasten her hair back behind her ear..."

He nods encouragingly, "Good...what else?"

"And she likes it when I call her my 'love'"

"Very true."

"And sometimes I catch her staring at my lips."

My father sips his scotch and studies me, smiling.

"You're missing a big one," he informs me.

Out of observations, I shrug.

"Your fingers, Reed."

"Seriously?"

I'm genuinely surprised.

"You can't have missed how dazed she becomes every time you play the piano," he laughs.

"I thought she was devastated by my talent!"

At that, he snorts loudly.

"I think she's too busy thinking of where she'd like those long fingers to focus on your musical prowess."

He glances at his own hands approvingly before swigging his drink and loosing another amused chuckle.

These long Whitney fingers haven't done very much so far, I think dejectedly. When my father's expression changes, presumably to mirror mine, I figured I'd better put it on the table.

"Dad, I've never..."

How can I put this?

"Neither of us has ever…taken our underwear off. She asks for more, but…"

"You don't want to hurt her?"

"That, and I don't want to screw it up."

"What makes you think you will? Is she more experienced than you?"

"No, we're both pretty inexperienced," I mumble.

"Then you'll learn together. Inexperience is nothing to be ashamed of."

He doesn't get it. I'm not explaining it well.

"When I'm with her, it doesn't seem like she's inexperienced. I know she seems all sweet and shy, but whenever we're together like that, she turns into this insatiable—"

…*beast*. I run my fingers through my hair in frustration.

"Has she ever had an orgasm?"

Huh. We've never explicitly talked about it, and I realize I don't know.

"If so, she'll be able to show you exactly how to touch her. If not, she may only have a vague idea of what it will take for her to achieve one. Either way, you should start by asking her to touch herself for you. But, pay attention—not just to how she touches her pussy, but to how the rest of her body plays in. Does she rub her breasts or tweak her nipples as she does it? Does she even touch her clit directly, or does she just touch around it? How light is her touch? How slow? Does she rub, pinch, or tap? Women aren't like us, Reed—to most of them, 'harder, faster, more' doesn't feel better."

I nod distractedly, visions of Aubrey touching herself infiltrating my mind and making my pants tight.

"And, when you do touch her, start with what you know she likes and do some exploration of your own. And I really mean an exploration—don't reduce her to her clit and her g-spot and be so laser-focused on getting her off that you ignore all the other touches that would bring her pleasure. I once heard of a woman who positively *came apart* when you stroked behind her knee as you sucked her clit."

Ugh.

His wistful smile confirms that, again, we're talking about my mother. I guess that's one way to take care of my hard-on.

Chapter Three

The Duck Pond

Aubrey

"Reed!" I gasp at the sensation of his palm grazing the side of my bare breast as he gently bites the juncture of my neck and my shoulder.

We lay on a picnic blanket near the duck pond at the college. We're in a hidden spot between the fence that surrounds the pond and some woods on the edge of the campus. Our lunch is untouched and our legs are intertwined. He's half on top of me, one thigh on the blanket, with the other sandwiched appealingly between my legs. My slow writhing tugs at his erection from where it is trapped between our

23

hips. The movement creates a delicious friction for me as well, and I'm sure he can feel my heat on his thigh through both of our jeans.

"Aubrey…" he growls, as if *I'm* the one who's sexing *him* to the edge of sanity.

It's not fair for any one being to hold such dominion over another, but, like this, Reed owns me. His scent alone bewitches me. Add in long, skilled fingers, the weight of his body, and the glorious things he can do with his mouth, and I'm gone. He's always made me lose control, but something about him lately is different. In two days, he's fanned the flames of my barely controlled fire into an inferno of unbridled lust.

"Please…" I beg hoarsely, for what I don't know.

He draws back to look at me, eyes dark and needful and his hair even wilder than usual.

"Tell me, love," he murmurs between kisses. "I want to know what you want."

The backs of his fingertips begin grazing my cheeks.

"I want to hear your fantasies," he continues, dropping tiny kisses along my jaw.

I barely hear my own soft whimper.

"I want to know how you touch yourself when you think of me." He traces his nose down the side of my neck.

"I want to memorize the look on your face and the sound of your voice when you come."

I moan as he kisses his way back up.

"Will you let me?" he whispers once he reaches my ear.

Reed

For once, I'm glad to be unraveled by want, to be so drunk with lust that I lose my filter. Thoughts of Aubrey getting herself off have infiltrated my mind from the moment my father planted the seed, and I'm just bold enough to ask. For a pregnant moment, I'm afraid that I've overstepped, but her whispered "yes" comes just in time. As I pull back to see her, her eyes foreshadow sacred revelations—of women's mysteries, of secrets and magic. The most luscious stab of fear slices through my desire as I realize she's about to show me.

My hands tremble subtly from the effort of my restraint as I help her off with her jeans. My cock clenches deliciously when I see that, indeed, the violet-colored lace bra I slid off of her earlier has delicate French-cut shorts to match. I slide my fingers up her leg in a motion that I hope is soothing before making them stop at the waistband of her little panties. Though my girl seems ready to go there with me, this is uncharted territory for us both. I stop, then—completely—searching her eyes again for the creep of apprehension. Her determined nod neutralizes the hesitant bite of her lip, and I slide the last piece of fabric off.

"Beautiful," I hear myself breathe, as Aubrey opens herself to me.

I'm kneeling by her feet, and she's bent her knees, and through the slight spread of her legs, I can see…everything. I feast my eyes first upon her pussy, noting how it is different, and more delicate, than the ones I've seen in porn. Though

Aubrey is well-groomed, she isn't shaved bare, and her little strip of curls looks soft. I spy her rosy clitoris near the top of her slit, and marvel at how the skin near her opening positively glistens. I drink in the rest of her, from her puckered areolae to the heated flush on her skin that belies them. By the time my eyes meet hers, she's writhing subtly upon the blanket—waiting, I realize, for me.

"Are you cold, love?" I ask, fairly certain of the answer.

Her teeth still worry her lip as she shakes her head.

"Nervous?" I whisper, less certain this time.

Her self-conscious nod relieves me.

"Me, too. You don't have to do this, Aubrey," I offer just as gently, letting her know with my eyes that things will be fine either way.

"I do this all the time," she admits, sending a jolt of bliss to my dick. "It's just…I've never let anyone watch."

My eyes shoot downward when I see her hand move. It travels slowly from where it sat on her hip, her middle finger leading a charge that ends on her darkened pink clit. Her breathing catches as she gives it two light strokes before pushing down toward her opening, before dipping a slender digit inside.

I quell the compulsion to sob with joy—I'm desperate to see her at work. I watch with rapt fascination at how she goes in only to her knuckle, how she pulses her finger slightly, almost imperceptibly, before withdrawing it languidly and dragging it up her slit. My fist tightens around her balled-up panties as her knees pigeon inward and she begins to stroke her inner labia with a gentle touch.

"You're so wet," I whisper in awe, my eyes still fixed on her center.

She doesn't answer me—only keeps on. Space and time drop away as she moves her hand, intermittently painting and dipping with her finger. We moan in unison when her left finger joins her right, first spreading the wetness around her lips and then double-teaming her clit. The surety of her movements and the finesse of her hands proves indeed that she does this often.

I make the mistake of glancing up at her face and find her mouth agape in unbridled pleasure.

"Aubrey—"I sob brokenly, for I am panting now.

But her eyes are on me, and my crotch.

It has escaped my notice that I'm stroking my hard-on through my jeans. By then, I'm too fucking far-gone to care. A cool breeze hits then, surprising us both, her breathless silence broken by her sudden whimper of pleasure.

"Help me," she pleads gently, reaching for my hand, pulling my whole body toward her.

I scoot in closer, her one leg between my knees, and let her steer my hand.

GentleGentleGentleGentleGentle, I have the presence of mind to remember. She takes my index finger straight to her opening and guides me slowly forth.

Hot…Wet.. Silk…

None of these words do justice to describing the feeling of being inside my Aubrey. We both exhale deeply once my finger is engulfed. Her walls tighten around me as she rotates my wrist until my palm faces skyward. She lets out a long, gratified wail as I slowly pull my finger out. We develop a fascinating rhythm. She teases her bud as I stroke her slowly from inside. I'm not totally sure I'm doing this right, but Aubrey's soft moaning and chanting—which seems to be escalating—indicates otherwise. A whimper rips from her, unbidden, as her fingers grasp my wrist to still my hand. I began to withdraw, worried I'm hurting her, but she holds me in place.

My eyes fly to her face in time to witness the magnificence of her orgasm. Fuck, I can feel her pulsing on my finger. She's all arching backs and helpless cries, all aftershocks and bonelessness, and a final indolent sigh.

By the time I remember my own arousal, what to do next turns out to be a moot point. I came in my fucking pants.

The moment my father sees my face, he ushers me right inside. As he strides wordlessly to grab two snifters from the bar (apparently troubled times call for cognac), I sink, defeated, into my wingback chair. Staring interminably into the fire, I revel in the liquor's burn. My dad's quiet solidarity, the way he knows when to let me come to him, gives me the space to work it all out. I finally gather the courage to speak.

"I think I need help with rule number two—not the

part about making her come, the part about making sure she does before me."

When I meet my dad's eyes, his smile is not mocking. Instead it seems to register…pride?

"So, I take it things went well yesterday?"

He must've misheard me.

I grumble, "Not as well as I'd hoped."

Scandalized that I'll have to say this out loud, I resolve to be blunt enough to only have to say it once.

"Dad…" I say gravely, "…there is no unit of measure small enough to describe how fast I came."

The man actually laughs—*laughs*—as I angrily blush with a depth that surely rivals my Aubrey's.

"But it sounds like *she* came?"

"Yes, but—"

He's not listening to me.

"And it was the first time you ever tried?"

"*Yes.*" I grind out, my voice now accusing, "*You* were the one who told me to have her show me."

Now I'm really pissed. Why are we reviewing things we both already know? And why does he seem almost gleeful?

"Son, do you know how many husbands can't make their wives come? How many women have never even had an orgasm? How many rely on toys and masturbation for whatever crumbs they can get?"

Wait, seriously? What kind of piss-ant husband can't make his wife come?

"Yet, you manage to find a woman who not only knows

her own body, but who trusts you enough to show you how to please her, and you get her off *the first time*?"

I guess when you put it that way...

"Aubrey seemed to like it," I admit cautiously, still a little upset.

"I'll just bet she did," he retorts cheekily, and lets out another little laugh. "You're a chip off the ol' block, son."

That was cheesy as hell, and I roll my eyes, but I might be smiling inside, just a little.

"So you want to talk stamina, then?"

"Please," I ask, calmer now.

I can't handle a repeat of today.

"How often to you jerk off?"

A week ago, this conversation would have scarred me for life, but it seems we've come a long way.

"Daily," I admit without hesitation.

"Well, there's your problem, son. You have to step it up."

For the next 20 minutes, he coaches me on timing and frequency, on the practice of backing myself off when I'm getting close. He warns me off of desensitizing creams, and supplements and pharmaceuticals, and tells me about something called a kegel (which he, for some reason, mentions aren't just for women). He says this is the hardest part for a teenager to master, but once I get it I'll be farther ahead than men much older than me.

I'm feeling much better about things by the time we finish our cognac, and thank him profusely as I stand to leave. He claps a reassuring hand on my shoulder as we stride toward the door.

"You did great, son. I'm beyond proud of you, not just for succeeding, but for having the courage to try."

"Thanks, Pop."

By then we're both grinning.

"Oh! Before I forget, there's something I want you to read before the next time we meet."

He steps back over to his desk and picks up a small white book that sits, ready, near one of the corners. I read the title aloud as he places it in my hand.

"*She comes first: The Thinking Man's Guide to Pleasuring a Woman?*"

He waggles his eyebrows.

"Take good care of it—that copy's got sentimental value."

I cringe, wondering whether I'll ever be able to look my mother in the eye again. With that, I beat a hasty retreat. I'll dive into the book tomorrow, but right now I'm exhausted. And my mind has already taken in enough new information for one day.

"Go get 'er, Tiger!" he calls as I walk up the stairs.

Chapter Four

The Parental Units

Preston

They should be back by now, I think impatiently, straining my eyes to see the far end of the driveway before glancing again at my watch.

It's been ten long days since I've seen my girls and they were due back home around three. I took the day off from the hospital and, too eager to sleep in, ran my errands this morning. The fridge is stocked with their favorite foods; fresh flowers grace every surface; I've chilled a bottle of Kate's favorite Fumé Blanc; and dinner is on the stove.

Wanting to be ready in case they got in early, I'd rushed

to my bedroom to groom: a close shave with my straight razor and a fingernail clip; a shower with sandalwood soap; the grey cashmere sweater that hugs my biceps and the blue jeans that sit just right on my hips. The house is squeaky clean, and so am I. All there is left to do is wait.

3:15 p.m.

And wait.

3:25 p.m.

And wait.

3:35 p.m.

And wait.

I feel small standing in my study, dwarfed by the tall palladium window, feel insignificant without her in this house. Though this is my family's estate—the house I grew up in—without her laugh, her touch, her smile, it doesn't feel like home. Certainly, things feel empty without my daughter, too. Despite her diminutive size, Nikki has quite a presence. Yet however much I've missed my daughter's light, I am bereft without my wife.

Where are they?

I finger the phone in my pocket, and consider giving them a call. I've already been teased twice by Nikki for being a Nervous Nellie, but my peace of mind means more than my pride. I get as far as unlocking the keyboard and scrolling to Kate's number when I hear the A4 on the driveway.

Now, I'm not one for running, but I'm out the door of my study in a flash. I manage to slow it to a brisk walk by the time I reach the foyer, manage not to swing the door open so hard as to take it off its hinges. Relief. Gratitude. Joy. Pride. I glow as my girls step out of the car. My heart melts—as it does every time—when Nikki runs to me and launches herself into my arms. I tamp down my sadness at the thought of her leaving for college next year. Some part of me will always see her as my little girl.

"We missed you, dad!" she enthuses, unaware of my grief.

"I missed you, too, squirt," I reply gruffly.

Kate's smile as she watches us is like the woman herself—knowing, precious and kind.

The blare of a car horn sends all of our heads turning to see the Jeep speed up the drive.

"Reed!" Nikki exclaims, abandoning me to greet her twin.

I close the distance to Kate then, a new lump forming in my throat as I collect my wife in my arms. It takes effort not to confess how much I've missed her, not to lose myself in her touch, not to kiss her the way that I've wanted. I settle for a caress to her face, a PG-13 kiss that won't scar the kids, and a deep, telling gaze into her lovely eyes.

"Mom..." Reed breathes a minute later, with a smile in his voice, coaxing her from my arms to pull her into his own embrace.

I feel blessed then, to have my whole family back together.

My family, together at last.

Kate

"Go ahead inside, Mom. Dad and I will bring in the bags," Reed smiles down at me.

How I love my gentle son's voice. I will always cherish the bonds Nikki and I forged on this trip, but I'm relieved to be home with my boys.

"They must've really missed us this time," Nikki whispers conspiratorially as we step into a sparkling clean house.

We giggle together, thinking of mother-daughter trips of years past, of coming home to a slew of well-intentioned gifts.

"Remember that time they tried to make Baked Alaska?" I recall with a raised eyebrow.

She snorts. "I remember them setting the kitchen on fire."

By then, we're both full-out laughing, but I quickly nudge Nikki in the side.

"Act grateful, honey," I chide gently, composing myself as I hear them coming in with our bags.

We spend the next few hours trading stories from our week. Preston catches us up on all the small-town gossip while Reed reports the latest from school. I tell the boys about the pieces we picked out on the two days we spent antiquing, and Nikki gushes about NYU. Reed speculates on which campus he'll like most when he and Preston make their own trip in the spring.

Their dinner is barely finished when the kids bee-line for the door. Nikki is ecstatic to see Jasper, and Reed is set on meeting Aubrey. The blush that colors my son's cheeks when he announces this fact does not escape me. I'll ask Preston about it soon.

"Why don't you let me do the dishes, my love?" he murmurs, reaching across the dinner table to hold my hand. We are alone at last. "It'll give you a chance to get comfortable," he reasons, smiling coyly and knowing fully that he fools no one with his ruse.

The kids will be gone for hours.

"I *could* stand to get out of these travel clothes," I muse, every bit as coy, squeezing his hand as I rise from my chair.

He is fascinating like this, all calm beauty on the surface when beneath, he boils like milk. One second you can barely recognize that he's heating; the next, he boils over, sudden and untamed. At times I prefer the wantonness of the overflow, and let him boil on high. At others I want low heat and patient stirring—the slow but constant burn.

What will it be tonight?

I wonder this as I climb the staircase, feeling Preston's eyes on my legs as they wear the hell out of sheer stockings and high-heeled shoes. The delicious unknown of my husband's plan steps with me into our gargantuan dressing room. We call it 'the closet'—it has been converted from a guest room to adjoin our bedroom suite. I designed the octagonal shape of the usable space and placed mirrors that allow me to see from any angle. Standing before the chest of drawers that holds my jewelry box, I take a moment to remove my earrings. I walk to my vanity and pick up my brush, mindful again of what he might have in store. Will he make slow, reverent love to me or will he fuck me with abandon? Will he slay me with laughter or astonish me to tears? Will he romance me first, relaxing me with a massage and feeding me dipped strawberries?

Mmmmm, strawberries...

My nipples harden at the recollection of the last time we played with that fruit.

Preston

I lean against the doorframe for minutes, watching her undress, uncaring of how the cold wine bottle chills my hand. I've planned to pour her a glass of wine and entice her to join me in our bath, to wash her gently before reacquainting her with our bed. I've planned to kiss, massage, and caress the travel-weariness from her body, to worship her for hours.

I won't make it that long.

This fact, I know, is shocking. Half the men my age can't even get it up, but my own sex life is raging. I'm one of few men I know who's still on my first marriage, who hasn't dabbled with mistresses or hookers—I actually want to fuck my wife. Twenty years of marriage and a libido like mine mean that I've been inside this woman a thousand times. Yet, just watching her, just being near her still makes me *so fucking hard. Stamina-crushingly* hard, since she's been gone for more than a week.

It's not just lust, though there's a healthy dose of that. Over the years it's become more. It is some greater love, the essence of which can never be captured in words. But so big is *it*, that it comes through in other ways—in touches, and gazes, and dreams.

I float towards her, discarding the wine and glasses atop a dresser along the way. She doesn't notice my presence until I'm upon her, my chest to her back, my breath on her ear, and my hardness against her hip. When I meet her eyes in the mirror, I see another profound truth.

I still have the same effect on her.

She's known what was coming. I've hunted her like this ten thousand times. She allows me to indulge my inner predator , and even enjoys the theater of me doing the taking. Yet, we both know that I, and not she, am the prey.

She owns me.

For all of my tutelage of Reed, we haven't yet gotten to the true nature of sexual control. I'm building him up now—emboldening him to claim his power. I have yet to tell him that, with the right woman, the power belongs to her. My Kate knows this, of course, as she gazes back at me. Knows how she makes me weak. Knows how she brings me to my knees for her, only for her. It's the most beautiful, frightening thing. It's the thing I can least control.

I break her gaze in the mirror to slide my hands up her hips, to sweep her silky hair over one shoulder. The first wave of gratification washes over me as I drink in a billow of her perfume. My steady surgeon's hands find the zipper of her dress and lower it languidly. I push the delicate fabric down from her shoulders and watch it pool at her feet.

"My love," I whisper as my head dips downward, my teeth delivering a hungry bite to a spot just behind her ear.

My hands return to her waist, caressing it for a brief, tender moment before pushing her shoulders roughly, in a way that coaxes her to fold at her hips. Her forearms fall, crossed, upon the vanity to support her. She drops the brush she's been using on her hair. Outside of a sharp breath, she's maddeningly silent. Years of being quiet for the benefit of the kids has necessitated our restraint. But however subtle, I can still hear her reactions, sense her whimpers and gasps and whines. If anything, the forced silence turns me on, as does the moment she loses the ability to hold it.

Admiring her in the few clothes that remain, my fingers itch to touch her thigh-high clad legs, to run the length of the filmy mauve thong that matches her bra and garter. I fall to my knees and pull her thong aside to lap greedily at her slit. Her pussy is truly a gorgeous thing in its texture and taste and smell. I lick—just lick—inside her warmth, but with a zeal and practiced finesse that leaves us both panting. Eating her from behind has made me into quite the tease, as my tongue can't reach her clit. I can, however, do something else she likes. Sitting on my heels, I pull slightly back, thumbing her ass cheek aside with one hand while I slide the finger of another into her pussy. I let my tongue (so lightly) graze her puckered hole, and she moans low and sultry divine.

Oh, God yes!

It sends a jolt through my dick every time I manage to elicit French whore sounds from my classy, demure wife. I lick her there again, deciding among several ways I want to make her come right now, before deciding she can wait a minute more. With almost inhuman speed, I pull her to the floor, place a throw pillow under her hips, and grab some lube from the vanity drawer. Seconds later, I'm sucking her clit while the finger of one hand languorously strokes her g-spot. I hold her in limbo for minutes, loving her nails on my scalp and the sounds she's making too much to let her fall. I wait until she's consumed, until she's thrown her head back in surrender and likely forgotten her own name. When I slick up an idle digit and slide it into her ass, my woman completely shatters. No longer able to control her voice, she lets out a soft, quivering scream. My wife is not a screamer, and on the rare occasion I turn her into one, I glow golden with pride.

Kate

By the way he slithers up my body so soon after I come, I

know he's too keyed up to stop. He usually gives us a minute in between rounds, but tonight he's aggressive and wild. I love when he can barely hold his control. I'm glad he's never truly crossed that line, but what a rush when he gets close. He's attacking me now, his tongue laving my body smartly between pinches and squeezes and bites. He rids me of my bra, but I know he'll leave the hose and shoes. My man is kinky like that.

I'm sure we look like the Tasmanian Devil as we race to take off his clothes. He's been wicked to entice me with those jeans. It's a curse and a blessing, the way men improve with age while women fight to hold on to whatever we have. I'd recognized how true this would be for us many years before, thanking the gods that he would not grow fat and complacent, gleeful that my desire for him would only grow with time. And it has. Preston owns me completely, and I am his willing slave.

He slides into me unexpectedly then, my walls clenching in anticipation, and I know I will come again soon. Nothing grips me harder than proof of his need and tonight his need is great. He curses in a whisper as we still to relish the sensation, like breathless silence after freshly fallen snow. But the throb is strong, our hearts beating where we meet, and soon I can't help but to move.

I rock into his hips, and he pulls back to look at me. He loves the smolder of my eyes as I writhe. He joins my rocking, of course, riding me like a pro jockey, and I watch for all his beautiful signs. The lulling of his eyelids, the staccato rhythm of his breath, that final battle between surrender and control. He's trying to make it last so I get to come once more.

Inspired by my imminent release, and wanting to witness his climax in all its splendor, I still his hips and roll him onto his back. He groans indulgently, control now gone, as I lower myself onto his cock. It's never long for either of us when I stroke him like this. My hair falls back to brush his knees. He fondles my waist with one hand and thumbs my clit with the other. I wrap my arm back behind me and let the back of my fingers whisper across his balls. I set a slow, maddening pace that touches me in just the right place and that keeps him on the edge. And then I wait for the snap of the last vestiges of his control. When he grabs my hips forcefully and starts fucking me from underneath—which he always eventually does—his zeal catapults me forth to my release.

I smile in satisfaction, relishing these final moments that he does me long, and hard, and deep. My man isn't a screamer, but this time his climax comes with a desperate, whimpered cry. Before he even catches his breath, he pulls me down to hug me fiercely.

And I think, *there's no place like home.*

Two hours later, we sit in a hot tub nursing cool glasses of wine. It had turned out to be the kind of night where things went backwards: a wanton romp on the closet floor led to sweet lovemaking on our bed. When I was completely sated, he'd massaged my feet before leaving me to rest. I awoke from my cat nap when he lifted me from the bed, laying me gently into a bath steeping with fresh sage from my garden. He slid open the windows that sat beside our soaking tub, inviting in the other smells of the forest. At last, he coaxed me forward so that he could take his seat behind me. We touched and petted for what felt like a long time, running the tap every so often to re-heat the water. Sometimes I dozed and sometimes we chatted. It felt absolutely divine.

"So I talked to Reed. About The Rules."

I smile lazily at Preston's attempt to sound nonchalant. He has dearly anticipated these talks with our son. His own father had been somewhat absent, and The Rules are among Preston's only conscious memories of bonding. When I mentioned two weeks ago that I thought Reed and Aubrey were having sex, Preston's eyes had shimmered with delight. That instant, he'd vowed to have a man to man with Reed while Nikki and I were gone.

"How'd he take it?"

My husband may be tactful and kind, but Reed is shy as hell. Preston chuckles, the rumble of sound from his chest vibrating through mine.

"You should've seen the look on his face the first time I said 'pussy.'"

I smile around my glass as I take a sip of wine. I can just imagine Reed's blush. Half the time, he's worse than Aubrey.

I chide gently, still amused, "You said you'd be easy on him."

"Not to worry. It took him a few days to get over the initial embarrassment, but now he's doing great."

"And, by great you mean…"

"You know I can't say too much."

At that, I roll my eyes.

Preston takes this "Whitney Men Wisdom" a little too seriously. He's been freakishly tight-lipped about The Rules. Why he thinks he can tell me anything new about the mysteries of a woman's body seriously escapes me. Yet, he guards this wisdom jealously. It seems a good guess that this has something to do with pride.

He'd rather I'd never learned that The Rules existed. He'd been forced to come clean some twenty years before. We were high school sweethearts, not unlike Reed and Aubrey. We were both each other's firsts. Back then, when I compared kissing notes with my girlfriends and it was clear their men knew nothing compared to mine, I threatened to leave Preston if he didn't tell me exactly how a self-proclaimed novice knew so many tricks. And so he told me The Rules existed, and explained how he came to know them. Outside of sharing his intention to tell Reed one day, that was all I knew.

"At least tell me whether my suspicion was correct."

"It was not. They're close, but their virtue remains intact."

Their virtue?

"Aubrey's too?"

That surprised me a little. More than once, I'd seen her look about ready to rape my son. Her sixteen-year-old lust reminded me of mine. I may have violated Preston once or twice.

"Would you rather it not?"

"I didn't mean it like that. She just strikes me as...*eager.*"

Preston chuckles again.

"Apparently she is," he murmurs. "It's got Reed a little spooked. Doesn't know what he's got, lucky bastard. Between his Whitney genes and a woman like her, with my tutelage, they will be magnificent."

I give him a loving, warning, nudge. *Humility, thy name is Preston.*

"Alright, Dr. Ruth, but can you please just give him some time, and room to come into his own? He's more sensitive than you were, Preston. Rome wasn't built in a day."

"Of course I'll give him time," he says, too innocently.

And I see it right then. This situation needs damage control.

"In the meantime, I'll speak with Aubrey."

It's time to extend my own feminine wisdom—to tell her what I know of "Whitney Love" and to pass on what my mother told me.

"And tell her what, exactly?"

He's proceeding with caution. *Wise, dear, very wise.*

"The Rules, of course. You didn't think we had rules of our own? You know I had a talk with Nikki."

"I thought you told her about babies and birth control. I didn't think you told her about *sex!*"

I shake with laughter, unable to speak. *My love, you are so naive.*

"Really, Kate," he scoffs, annoyed no doubt by my

laughter and the thought of me having a similar talk with Nikki. "Doesn't Aubrey have a mother of her own?"

"Aubrey's mother lives over 3,000 miles away," I remind him. "And, didn't you have a talk with Jasper?"

He says nothing for a moment. He knows he's beat.

"Yes, dear. I suppose I did."

Chapter Five

Balinese Worm Tongue

Preston

"Sleep, my love," I whisper to Kate with a smooth of her hair and a kiss to her brow, though her whine of protest implores me to stay.

I'd loved her thoroughly (if not relentlessly) for each of the three nights and two mornings she's been back home and I know my wife is tired. Wanting nothing more than to drift off with her, I linger for a moment hoping I'll hear Reed's engine coming up the drive. But he isn't due home yet, and if I stay in bed I'll fall asleep, and one of us always makes sure the kids get home alright. Tucking the covers around her after I slip out of bed, I blow the candles out and give her a final kiss.

I wash up a little and pick up the room, saving Kate the trouble of tidying up in the morning. After slipping on striped gray silk pajama pants and a fitted v-neck undershirt, I quietly exit our room. Closing the door behind me, I stride toward the stairs, my footfalls silent on thick carpet. Just as I reach the top of the steps, I hear Reed walk inside.

I watch my son as he closes himself in and falls back against the door. His eyes are closed, his mouth curved in a crooked grin and he lets out an indulgent sigh. I smile a little smile of my own.

Looks like we both got some tonight.

"Did you and Aubrey get in some good studying?" I ask, taking to my descent of the stairs.

I don't bother hiding my smirk, so he doesn't bother lying. Deepening the angle of his grin as he slowly opens his eyes, he just shakes his head.

"But, I take it you kids had fun, *whatever* you did."

His eyes have followed me to the foot of the stairs.

"Dad, I think I'm in love."

His expression is still dreamy, and I can only chuckle.

"I thought we'd already established that."

"Not just with Aubrey, dad. I've been reading that book you gave me. I've been practicing what it says."

"And?"

He doesn't even find it in him to blush.

"And, I can't stop licking her pussy."

Reed

"She Comes First: The Thinking Man's Guide to Pleasuring a Woman" had turned out to be worth its weight in gold. Given my stamina problems I figured I'd better get good at pleasing Aubrey. This book had everything, from the misunderstood anatomy of the vagina, to the female orgasm, to notes on technique and timing. It went beyond mechanics and elevated the discussion to cunnilingus as a creative art. I read it in a single sitting and got over my intimidation quickly. I tried what I'd learned on Aubrey the very next day. That was two days ago, and ever since then, I couldn't get enough.

"She loves it, Dad. I wanted her to like it, but…"

But the little minx fucking loves it.

We're in the study by now, in our regular seats, drinking a very nice port.

"I mean, I fumbled a little at the beginning until I got my bearings." I admit. "But, then I hit a groove, and figured out what I was doing and it drove her fucking wild."

I look at him earnestly, then.

"And now she begs me, Dad. Begs me to let her come. I've never felt so powerful in my life. And the way *she* tastes…"

When my dick twitches in memory of Aubrey's delectable bouquet, I figure I'd better rein it in. I know I'm probably babbling, or saying too much, but I can't stop the words from spilling forth. Licking Aubrey's pussy is my favorite new thing to do and I owe my father big for even knowing how.

"I'm thrilled things are going so well, son. It came to my attention that covering so much ground in such a short time might be too much, too soon."

Is he kidding? Half the time I don't know whether to hug him for telling me all this now or punch him in the face for not doing it sooner.

"So, what's next? Do you want me to keep going with the rules, or do you want to stay on oral sex for awhile? An old swami taught me something called the 'Balinese Worm Tongue'. Your mother still sends him a holiday card."

I roll my eyes in silent surrender to these references about my mom. I'm slowly accepting the obvious and since her return, I've seen all the signs. The way she and my dad had both gone to bed early every night but came downstairs tired and happy every morning now makes sense. When I manage to ponder my parents' sex life without thinking about it too hard, I like that my mom has someone as devoted as my dad.

"Uh, maybe next time on the Balinese Worm Tongue…" That actually sounds kind of scary. "There's something else Aubrey is begging for and I don't know how much longer I can head her off."

"What's that, now?" He looks at me patiently as he takes a sip of his port.

"She wants to return the favor. She keeps bugging me to let her suck my…" I trail off, shifting self-consciously.

"And, you don't let her?"

Somewhat ashamed, I shake my head. He looks at me incredulously for a long moment before closing his eyes and pinching his nose in his fingers. When he speaks, his voice is dangerously low.

"The beauty of The Rules, son, is that they can be added onto and modified to instruct the wisdom of future Whitneys. Until tonight, there were a total of nine. But, tonight a new rule is born."

I shift uncomfortably in my seat as his eyes bore into mine.

"Can you guess what rule ten is, Reed?"

Now I'm afraid to speak.

"If the woman to whom you are committed begs to give you a blow job, for the love of God, you are to *take it*."

He makes it sound so simple. Of course I want to take it!

"But, Dad, what if—" I stammer helplessly. "What if something goes wrong?"

"Such as…"

"Like me losing control or coming all over her face or…" I gulp, then whisper, "Dad, what if she bites it?"

He looks at me incredulously for another moment before his lips quiver and he laughs. He has the decency to cover his mouth with his fist, but still.

"Glad I amuse you…" I sulk, putting down my drink.

He pulls himself together.

"She's not a vampire, son. I don't think she's going to bite you."

I look at him skeptically.

"And there's a universal signal for not coming all over her face. When it's almost time, give her a little nudge. Push her shoulder back or pull back on her hair and tell her you're about to come. She'll get out of the way if that's what she wants."

I nod reluctantly, supposing it makes sense, but a few minutes later, I'm still feeling sullen.

"Is there something else?"

His voice is concerned. If I'm honest, the answer is yes.

"Things are going so well now, and I seem to be making her happy…"

"And you're wondering why you can't just let things stay the way they are?"

I nod with dejection.

"Right now, she thinks I'm a sex god. I kind of want to keep it that way. For the first time I actually know what I'm doing."

His face softens and his eyes become wise and I know he'll say just the right thing.

"Reed, suppose Aubrey did bite you—by mistake, of course. Do you think you would love her any less?"

I shake my head.

"What would you do?"

"I'd forgive her, and be patient with her and help us learn together."

"That's the important part, son. You and Aubrey are in this together. And as long as you keep sharing your ups and downs, you'll be amazing."

I nod, knowing he's probably right, but still chagrined by the idea of letting go.

"And so goes another of The Rules, son: learn to give and take."

Chapter Six

Man Logic

Kate

I give Aubrey a warm hug as she approaches the front door, the first of many attempts to ease her nerves. I've always been welcoming of her role in my son's life but we've never spent much time alone. However affable I'd been when I called her that week, the summons to join me for lunch had been abrupt. I hadn't lied when I said I wanted us to get to know one another better, but I think she'd sensed I have something I want to discuss.

"Is there anything I can help with?" she asks, following me into the kitchen.

I shake my head. "It's all done. The croissants are just warming in the oven."

I grab a mitt and reach in to remove the buttery bread, making quick work of slicing each one in half and putting on just the right amount of chicken salad. Topping the mixture with watercress and replacing the top half on each sandwich, I set them down next to the taro chips I baked on the set breakfast table that overlooks the garden.

"I love chicken salad?" she smiles widely, eyeing the plate.

"Reed mentioned it was one of your favorites," I smile kindly.

I motion for her to sit before I do the same, and I request that she please go ahead and dig in.

"Thank you for having me over for lunch, Mrs. Whitney," she says politely, after complimenting my cooking. "It was nice of you to invite me."

I remember what it was like to be on my best behavior for Preston's parents, even when I was fucking their son.

"Please, Aubrey. Call me Kate. Mrs. Whitney was my mother-in-law, and she didn't like me very much."

Aubrey's well-mannered chewing abates long enough for her to look genuinely surprised.

"She thought I was bad for her son," I clarify, knowing that, one day, I'll tell her the story.

She looks around my kitchen and out to my garden.

"But you're, like, the perfect wife."

I laugh so hard at that, that she starts laughing, too and

it begins to break the ice. From there, the conversation flows. She asks me how I came to be the curator at a museum and I learn about her love for literature and her dreams to write. When she talks about she and Reed I learn little tidbits about my son that he's too busy to tell his poor mother. She speaks of him with fond animation and I find myself eating these little morsels up.

When I comment that I've noticed that she and Reed are serious, she seems to have anticipated the observation, affirming strongly how much she loves him. Though college applications aren't due for another three months, she admits they've talked about applying to the same schools. She looks relieved when I bring up the fact that Preston and I shared an alma mater. Finally ready to strike, I wait until she's chewed what is in her mouth. I don't want the poor girl to choke.

"So tell me, Aubrey. Did the multi-orgasmic fingers and magical tongue get passed down from my husband to Reed?"

When she chokes a little anyway, I just smile and continue.

"No need to be shy. I'm his mother, but I'm not blind. I'd be shocked if you could keep your hands off of him. And he practically salivates when you're in his presence, so I doubt he's keeping his hands off of you."

Her cheeks are the color of a pomegranate. She's more flustered than I had anticipated.

"Either you're mortified by the question or you're blushing deeply at the memory of my son making you come."

Pomegranate turns to raspberry.

"So, which one is it, dear?"

I pat her hand comfortingly, and laugh when she squeaks out her answer.

"Both."

Aubrey

"I don't mean to embarrass you," Kate says soothingly after I make the most mortifying confession of my life. "But, your own mother is far away, and I don't know how candidly you talk."

Her eyes are kind and she seems sincere, and, to be honest, her words strike a chord.

"Not very often," I admit, still blushing. "And, as you might imagine, leveling with The Chief is not an option."

Kate nods again. "I think I understand."

I wring my hands restlessly under the table, wondering what she wants me to say.

"You and Reed love and respect each other, Aubrey. Whatever you do together, there's no reason to be ashamed. From our perspective, you and Reed are lucky to have one another as your firsts. Preston was my first, and I was his, and we were both younger than the two of you."

Interesting.

But I'm still skeptical. Because Kate Whitney is the polar opposite of my own free-loving, bohemian mother. I'd never have turned to either of them on my own for advice about love, albeit for very different reasons.

"So you approve?"

She smiles.

"We'd rather make it safe for you than to shame you into hiding it away."

"Uh…thanks?"

I cringe when I hear my tone. It hadn't been meant as a question. Kate pats my hand again.

"Come, Aubrey. The sun is out for once. Why don't we go for a walk?" She pours us tea from an infuser filled with herbs so fresh that I know they must be from her garden, and we start out the kitchen door.

The Whitney property is expansive. It takes a few minutes to traverse her impressive garden and find ourselves on a gravel path. I listen to the pebbles crunch under our feet as we take our leisurely walk.

This should be awkward, but Kate's quiet manner is contagious. Somehow she's succeeded at instilling me with a sense of calm. Reaching the clearing that holds the oversized garden chess game, we finally settle on an old stone bench.

"I trust that health class and the Internet have given you a sense for what goes where," Kate begins again with a little smile.

"Yeah, well beyond that, they pretty much left us on our own," I say half under my breath.

She takes a long sip of her tea before setting it down on the bench.

"If you have questions, I hope you'll consider asking. The clearer you are on exactly what to expect, the better it'll be."

I let the sides of the mug warm my nervous hands, and stare into the clear, fragrant liquid. It takes me not seconds, but two or three minutes, to gather the courage to ask.

"You probably know this already, but Reed is..." I lower my already weak voice, "—pretty *big*. And I know he'd never hurt me on purpose, but...I'm almost sure he will."

I look up at her nervously, biting my lip, still half-expecting this to all be a trap.

"He probably will," she admits with a rueful smile. "But the pain will be worse if your muscles are tense. It'll get better with time but at the beginning, remember to relax and have him go slow."

Slight distress crosses her face.

"And, I won't lie to you, Aubrey—you may be disappointed. It'll be hard for him to last the first few times. Beyond learning stamina, he needs to figure out how to make you come that way, and it's bound to take him some time."

I nod, and take a thoughtful sip.

"But there are plenty of other things to keep you busy. Before...it sounded like Reed was doing well in other areas?"

My blush returns with a fervor. She lifts her cup once more and I think I see a smile hidden behind a lengthy sip.

"Reed is amazing," I admit. "More proof of his perfection," I mumble in a lower voice, but Kate hears me.

She casts me a sympathetic look and I feel a little bit childish for sulking.

"He only wants you to *think* he's perfect, Aubrey. The truth is, he's just as scared as you."

"Scared *of* me is more like it. He never lets me reciprocate." I lower my eyes in shame. "I think I'm doing something wrong."

I hear Kate put down her own cup again before she pulls mine out of my hand, setting the ceramic down with a soft clink upon the stone.

"Aubrey, I love my son and all of his quirks, but even I know he is obsessed with control. Has it occurred to you that he might slow things down because your reciprocation would feel so good, it would make him lose his shit?"

My eyes fly back to her face and my jaw drops straight down. Hearing a woman who prunes her rosebushes in a skirt and heels ask me in dulcet tones to consider whether fondling her son would make him "lose his shit" is just too much.

"Uh…" I stammer helplessly.

"I don't mean to be crass, dear, but if you've never gotten it stuck in a zipper, stroked it until it chafed, or bitten down on it too hard, you're not doing anything wrong."

What does she mean 'bitten down *too hard*'? Why would I ever bite it?

"Which only leaves the possibility that Reed is scared of embarrassing himself in front of you, Aubrey. He's scared he'll come too soon."

"But isn't that kind of the point?" I blurt, forgetting my couth but remembering my voice.

Kate only gives a contrite shake of her head before pinning me with a serious look.

"There is no making sense of man logic, Aubrey. If you learn nothing else today, learn that."

Kate

She looks dejected and I'm sorry to be the bearer of bad news, but someone had to be frank with her about the fragility of the male ego. The Whitney men, with their cool composure, can be particularly deceptive. Aubrey deserves the truth.

"So, what, I have to just…wait?"

The more I align her expectations with reality, the better it will be.

"Aubrey, a man's ego is a delicate thing—especially when it comes to sex. They all want to be stallions in bed, but they can't get there without a lot of feedback from us. The secret is, you have to find ways to coach them that don't make them feel like less of a man. Reverse psychology might be the best approach if confrontation isn't working."

She chews on her lip, thinking about this for a minute. I can see the wheels turning in her head.

"Reverse psychology, like, convince him I *don't* want to do it?"

That might be interesting.

"Hmmm…that's not quite what I meant. You need to say something that will play on his desire to satisfy *you* so that he lets you satisfy *him*. It might work if you told him you have a fantasy about having him in your mouth and that you love to watch him come."

I'm pleased when, instead of blushing or looking embarrassed by my forwardness, the corner of her mouth turns up in a devious smile.

Looks like we're making progress.

"So, basically, I should trick him?"

"It'll work like a charm," I confess, "…and not just in bed. You'd die if you saw the ugly clothes Preston picks up off the rack when we go shopping. But he *buys* whatever I tell him makes me hot."

She giggles.

"And when he started his residency? That was the absolute worst! His feet got so calloused and rough from all the hours of standing. So I told him I developed a foot fetish, and he started sneaking off to get pedicures."

By then I'm laughing too.

"You tricked Dr. Whitney into getting *pedicures*?"

Her eyes are as wide as saucers.

"And I did it without an iota of guilt. You know, men have their own wisdom for dealing with us, too. Turnabout is fair play."

…which reminds me of something she said earlier.

"And, Aubrey? That thing you said about Reed being

perfect?" I shake my head. "Let's just say he's getting at least as much help as I'm giving you."

Realization dawns on her face as she figures out that someone is coaching Reed. I put my arm around her shoulder in a motherly gesture.

"One day—not now, but years from now—remind me to tell you about The Rules."

Chapter Seven

Like Sands Through The Hourglass

Aubrey

I've taken to wearing skirts. Indian summer has followed us well into October, and they make sneaking off with Reed much easier. And when I say "sneaking off", I mean cutting class regularly and hiking to a private little spot in the woods behind the school.

Far past the little cove where all the stoners get high, and way out of the way of blow job rock, is a tiny, unshaded clearing nestled in a natural circle of shoulder-high boulders. An old, fallen tree lays rotting and mossy nearby, part of it and the boulders staying warm and dry. A small patch of sun shines through most afternoons.

We've been here more than a few times since things started getting intense, since Reed started treating my hoo-ha like the Bellagio buffet and since his mother wore pearls and served tea while talking about the family jewels. I'm not complaining, exactly. While other high school girls suffer through fumbling make-out sessions that are, in all likelihood, anticlimactic, Reed's lithe fingers and deft tongue give me more big Os than a dozen Tim Hortons.

But, there's another important difference between the other girls and me—their sweaty-palmed boyfriends are begging for more. I, meanwhile, have managed to fall in love with the only eighteen-year-old boy in the history of the world who is holding on to his v-card.

It consumes my every thought. Time apart from Reed is spent not working on college applications, but silently bargaining with the God of Getting Some to please, just let me touch his cock. Don't laugh. Just because I haven't really seen it yet doesn't mean I don't know what it can do. If it has even half the talent of his other parts, selling my virgin soul to have at it will have been a fair price.

But, my prayers haven't been answered and even Kate's practical advice isn't getting me far. I've tried reverse psychology. It turns out Reed isn't as smart as he looks. My brilliant, thick-headed boyfriend has been letting me closer to the goods, but at this rate, we'll be in college before I get a good look.

Maybe I shouldn't complain.

Any progress is good progress, I suppose. And it beats the hell out of going backwards. Over the weekend he'd let me unzip his pants and fondle him through his underwear while he ate me out. But, instead of mollifying me, it only prompted me to want more, more of those primal sounds he'd made, more of him pulsing in my hand. When he'd warned that he was going to come, I'd snuck my hand past his waistband for the last couple of strokes. Reed's dick was hot, silky heaven.

God, I'm such a horny bitch, I think as I shift a little in my seat, letting my eyes fall upon Reed's studying form. His left pointer finger holds a spot on the page in his math book while he works a problem in his notebook with his right. A wave of heat (the angry kind) crashes over me. How can Reed focus on Calculus when every other boy his age (and half the girls in the room) are surely thinking about sex?

Enough.

And, I *have* had enough, I realize. Waited long enough. Been understanding enough as I let Reed set the pace. Now, the time has come. It's not like I want to drown his puppy, for fuck's sake! I just want to make him feel good. As good as he makes me feel. Maybe even better.

Reed

Library instead of lunch.

I take a break from studying Calculus problems so I can

surreptitiously read Aubrey's text. We aren't supposed to be texting in study hall, but this is one of many rules that Aubrey and I ignore. We'd started the semester sitting next to each other, but the teacher had had to "separate" us for disrupting things. Now we text instead of taking. We've even sexted on occasion. It makes me wonder sometimes, how teenagers flirted with one another in school before the advent of smartphones.

Not hungry?

I've kind of been hoping that, for lunch, we'll head out to that place in the woods. We've had some epic make-out sessions there these past couple of weeks.

Our "study date" after school? We're not gonna study :)

I try to look outwardly normal as, inwardly, I surrender to what has gone from a hopeful to a justified boner. At least I have another 20 minutes of class before I need it to go away.

Fuck, I think, already imagining what might happen after school. After the last little talk with my dad, which had ended with some pointers on technique, I feel much closer to letting Aubrey have her way. I've been working on my stamina and feel closer than ever to being able to take the next step without completely embarrassing myself. Does Aubrey want it to happen today?

Study hall drags on, but at least I knocked out most of the project I'm supposed to be working on after school. But, in bio, I can't help but notice that Aubrey looks a little distracted. Her eyes are forward, but her face is flushed and she has a strange little smile on her face. So I write a new note on the corner of my paper and slide it her way.

Care to share with the class?

After she reads it, I look at her meaningfully and raise an eyebrow. But instead of grabbing the notepad and sharing her thoughts, which Aubrey always does when I ask, she shrugs (rather coyly, I think), blushing ever so slightly as she trains her eyes back toward the front of the class.

Aubrey, what are you thinking about? I write back urgently.

I've sprung wood yet again by the time I pass her this second note. She keeps her attention upon the paper for a torturous minute, before revealing the truth with her eyes. The look she gives me starts out sexy guilty dangerous, then turns predatory, almost fierce.

By then I'm not even pretending to pay attention to the lecture. I am, instead, rapt by her eyes traveling slowly down my jaw, then across length of my fingers, before falling to my lap. And, when she bites her lip then it's not shy, or cute or nervous.

Her gaze lingers, and I'm frozen, breathless to her every move. In that moment I feel that I'd do anything she asked, right here in bio, in front of everyone. But she doesn't ask. She just stares at my cock for way longer than is appropriate before putting pen to paper and writing back a note of her own.

I think we both know the answer to that.

It's possible that I actually moan at some point during the reading of her note. I'm too worked up to check whether anybody noticed.

Quietly, I take Aubrey's left hand, which is resting on her thigh, and cover it with mine. Ever so slowly, so as not to be discovered, I slide it on top of my erection. It's not that I want my girlfriend to fondle me in bio—rather, I have to teach her a lesson about what a note like that can do to a guy. I have zero hope of going about the rest of my day without a conspicuous boner.

"You're in so much trouble," I lean into her ear and deliver a low growl that only she can hear.

The little vixen's response is to give my cock a squeeze. I myself do more than squeeze it in an out-of-the-way bathroom right after class. I more than squeeze it again when I take another bathroom break eighth period to rub one out.

The afterschool study session is at my place. My parents are pretty liberal to begin with when it comes to having Aubrey in my room, but it doesn't matter today anyway—they're both working late.

"What the fuck were you thinking?" I demand when we finally reach my bedroom, divesting her of her backpack as I silently vow to kiss the sly little smile from her face. I don't back up an inch, my tall frame towering over her as I make to walk her backward toward the bed. Verbal foreplay is one thing, but doing what she'd done and me not being able to do anything about it for four fucking hours is another.

"Not so fast," she feints, poking her finger in my chest just as she ducks her head to dodge what was going to be a serious kiss. "You're absolutely sure your parents won't come home?"

"Positive," I murmur, bowing my head towards her once again. This time her whole palm firmly pushes my chest, keeping me at bay.

I try not to groan as I take a step back.

Please don't change your mind, please don't change your mind, I pray-chant in my head.

"Good," she says, a wicked smile forming on her face. "Then you can be as loud as you want when I make you come."

Shit—we're really going to do this! I think I might have just swooned. In a manly way, of course. I hear metal against metal, the clanging of my belt as Aubrey unfastens my pants. It jolts me back to the present. I clench my fists to keep from reaching out, from stopping her hands as I've done so many times before. I think of my father and the tenth rule, tell myself to man up, and jump into the abyss.

It's dreamlike—allowing her to turn us around, to sit me on the bed and take off my pants. It is every fantasy come true: watching her sink to her knees before me, seeing her flip her hair to the side, feeling her breath tickle my skin before her tongue peeks out.

"Oh, God…"

My fists dig in to clench my bed sheets. My voice doesn't sound like my own. I absolutely cannot watch this if I want to maintain control.

I squeeze my eyes shut and my head falls back. Her hands are so small. Her touch, so light and unsure. Her tongue is so warm, its fascinating texture scintillating my hyper-sensitive flesh. And when her tentative fingers slide down to fondle my balls, I discover the meaning of ecstasy. I also discover that I'm capable of making a noise that sounds like a wounded mountain lion.

"Shit, did I do something wrong?"

It's not so much Aubrey's voice that permeates my haze as it is the cool air that hits the head of my cock when her lips leave their rightful home. I want to wrap my fingers around the back of her head and shove my dick back into her hot little mouth, and more deeply this time. If I were thinking clearly, I'd be a bit scared of myself. This is making me rather…feral.

"Fuck no, don't stop," I plead instead, stopping just short of begging a pretty please with sugar on top. I need her mouth back on me more than I need air to breathe. I hope my words persuaded her, but just in case, I glance down to throw her a reassuring look.

Wow, I shouldn't have done that, I think, taking in dark lashes against flushed cheeks, and the matching pink of her swollen lips. Watching her mouth descend upon me a second time, more firmly, more confidently, completely does me in. I can't warn her. There's no time. I come spectacularly, right in Aubrey's mouth.

Aubrey

In the two weeks since he's started letting me near little Reed, my control freak boyfriend has become quite the little whore. He can barely keep his pants on. Every time we're alone, his eyes light up with hope that I might give a repeat performance of that first time in his room.

I've more than thrice obliged him, suddenly understanding both sides—especially why he kept wanting to do it to me. Once I got past that first brackish mouthful of "Essence of Reed," I started tasting something different when I had him in my mouth: I discovered the taste of power, and I rather liked the finish.

It excites and awes me all at the same time—witnessing his pleasure is unbearably sexy. His voice, the way his hands thread in my hair, and even the raggedness of his breath get me as hot (if not hotter) than the most intimate touches. Seeing how vulnerable he is in these moments, and the moments after, fills me with gratitude and wonder. I finally know what all the hype is about. I see how people get too caught up in the moment to remember condoms. I have a new perspective on affairs and one night stands and how one thing could lead to another. Some moments, some connections between two people, take on lives of their own.

And speaking of that one thing and that 'nother…I can sense us getting close. Now that Reed is no longer shy of me touching him, our make-out sessions are getting pretty heavy. We're two kids in love whose parents spend an extraordinary time away from home. It's only a matter of time.

Chapter Eight

The Chief

Reed

"Chief Truman!" I say with enough surprise in my voice to immediately regret it. But I get it together. "What a pleasant surprise."

"It's nice to see you again, Reed," he says in that cryptic way he always does. Not coldly, but not warmly either, the scrutiny of his gaze betraying the friendliness of his words. I don't, nor have I ever, gotten the feeling that this man likes me.

He has no legitimate claim to having anything against me, of course. I've never been in trouble at school, let alone with the law. I get good grades. I always have Aubrey home by curfew. He's never seen or heard that I treat Aubrey with anything but the utmost respect, because I always do. But I'm dating his teenage daughter. And part of me knows that's enough.

"She's still getting ready. Said she'll be down in fifteen minutes." he explains, motioning for me to follow him into the dining room. It strikes me as peculiar, as we've only sat together in the living room before. "It's been awhile since we talked," he remarks a bit more lightly, and I know he's up to something. A second later, I see there's a disassembled gun laying on a cloth on the table.

Involuntarily, my eyes, look toward the stairs in a futile hope that Aubrey will appear that second, sparing me from whatever tense conversation is to come. But I can hear the shower running, which means that fifteen minutes may be optimistic. She could've at least warned me with a text.

"Please, sit." The chief motions to a chair directly in front of him and for a moment, I envision being shot, execution style. I gulp as I imagine blood and brain matter splattered all over the prettily papered walls.

"Thank you," I say politely, my voice catching a bit. When the corner of his mouth lifts at the sound, I know he knows he's got me.

"Do you shoot guns, Reed?"

I shake my head honestly as I watch him pick up some sort of polishing cloth. "My father owns a few pistols, but I don't think he's ever shot them. They're on display as collector's items," I ramble.

"You're missing out," he murmurs, and I watch with sick fascination as he slowly begins to reassemble the gun. I wasn't lying—I know nothing about guns, but whatever this is, it is clearly a serious weapon. Its heavy black metal is a far cry from the pearl-handled antiques mounted in glass cases on the walls back home.

"There's something satisfying about pulling the trigger. It's a rush to feel how much power you hold in your hand. It kicks back good after you fire it, but the pressure you put on the trigger doesn't take much."

I gulp.

"Is that your service weapon?" I manage, using jargon I've heard on crime dramas.

"This beauty?" he looks at me like I'm a little bit crazy. "I guess you really don't know guns. This is a modified Walther PPK. It's the same gun James Bond uses. It's my own personal weapon. I've got it engineered to go off on a hairline."

Pushing the chief's spy fantasy out of my mind, I bring up another point that only occurs to me because I've watched a lot of television. "I thought engineering the trigger was illegal."

His smile looks macabre to me. "The rules are different for me. Remember? I'm law enforcement."

"Have you ever…" I gulp. "Used it?"

"Discharged it? Yes. At the range. But never on the streets. But I like knowing it's here for me to use if I ever have to."

I laugh nervously. "This is a small town. I doubt anyone would be stupid enough to try you."

We're both looking at his fingers as they work at loading bullets into the magazine. He's just slid the clip into the handle when he looks me dead in the eyes.

"You'd be surprised."

I'm absently aware that the shower is still running as we stare each other down. He's silent for so long that it dawns on me: this isn't mere intimidation—it's a test. If he only wanted to scare me, he'd keep talking—about what a good shot he is, and how he could kill someone and make it look like an accident. But he's doing none of that. He's standing his ground, but at some point, I can tell he's waiting for me. And I know what I have to say.

"It occurs to me…" My voice is weaker than I want it to be, and I clear my throat before continuing. "That I've never told you my intentions when it comes to your daughter. I can tell you about them if you'd like, but I should warn you—they're not innocent."

The briefest rays of respect that dawn in his eyes are quickly replaced by shock. I don't miss the way his grip on the handle of the gun tightens and I half-expect him to point the thing at me.

"This isn't a high school romance for me, sir. I love your daughter. More than that, I respect her. I may be young, but I'm not too young to know that I'll ask you for her hand in marriage one day."

I choose my next words carefully, because I don't want

to outright lie to him but I do want him to know I'm not just some horny kid looking to deflower his daughter.

"I know that it's not my job yet—at least not officially—to protect her well-being. But looking out for her is a part of me. Making sure she's safe is ingrained in everything I do."

I might be holding my breath as I wait, reading him for a reaction, hoping to God he won't make me say any more than that. But he's winning this standoff and I grasp for something—anything more—to convince him I'm worthy.

"Ready to go?" Aubrey practically flies into the room. Her hair is still wet from the shower. Her eyes widen as she takes in the scene.

"Really, Dad?" She gives the Chief a reproachful look before tugging my hand and trying to pull me off of the chair. But it would be rude, not to mention cowardly, to walk away too abruptly.

"Your father and I were just talking," I offer.

"I think we're all done," the Chief remarks neutrally, probably for Aubrey's benefit.

I do rise from my chair then and look him right in the eye. "Sir, I meant what I said."

Aubrey

I need an assist.

It's 9:35. I've just come back from being out with Reed.

After passing my father's not-so-subtle inspection for evidence of drinking, drugs or sex on my way inside, I've decided it's time to call my mother. I rarely call her outside of emergencies like this, but I know she will understand what has become our shorthand. On the rare occasion that my dad starts acting weird, she's my first call. They were only together for a few years, but somehow she still knows him better than anyone else.

"Uh-oh," she says, not waiting for me to greet her when I pick up the phone a minute later. I knew she'd be awake. Not only is she in a different time zone—she's a hospital nurse. Her shifts have her going in at two in the morning.

"He's crazy," I begin.

"Who?"

"Your ex husband," I say with emphasis. "Reed wouldn't talk about it, but when I came downstairs to go on the date he deliberately made me late for, Dad was cleaning his guns on the dining room table."

At this, my mother laughs openly, to which I mutter a quiet "Not helpful." And then, "It was your swell idea to procreate with a cop and doom your daughter to a life of overprotection."

"Oh, honey...he wasn't always a cop. He of all people should know what it's like to be a teenager in love."

"But he's scaring Reed away," I practically whine, flopping down on my bed. I've been wearing Reed down for months, and it feels like one scared straight warning from the chief is jeopardizing my plan.

"Greg wasn't born yesterday. He knows he can't stop a moving train."

"Well, he's making a good show of trying. Did I tell you he's stopped going fishing on Saturdays? And that he's developed a habit of coming back early at times when he said he wouldn't be home? Next thing you know, he'll send a medieval tailor to fit me for my chastity belt…"

I'm joking. Kind of. And I expect my mother to laugh, but her solemn words take me by surprise.

"Trust me on this one. One day you'll be thankful to have been raised by a man who cared enough to protect your virtue."

Shit.

I don't know my mother's whole story, but the older I get, the more breadcrumbs she lays down. Between those, and things I've pieced together myself, I'm sure of a few things. I know her life has been a study in looking for love in all the wrong places. That she's moved on from men, and even from me, because she's never found whatever it is she needs. And I know my cold-as-ice grandfather had something to do with that.

But she's right—I am lucky to have a dad like Greg. He's raised me alone from the time I was three, and he's always put me first. Without me in the picture, I'm pretty sure he'd have remarried, and followed more of his own dreams. But he'd always reminded me that just the two of us was more than enough.

"I *am* thankful," I relent. "But I'm not a little girl

anymore. I just…wish I knew what the hell he's trying to do."

"He's holding on to what little control he wants you and Reed to think he has, for the short remainder of time he'll have it. It's part of the process."

"Of making my life miserable?" My voice is sad now.

"Of saying goodbye to his little girl."

I sigh, because she's probably right. For all her imperfections, she's always right about things like this. And what she's saying makes sense. Last month, and about three years later than my mother had, my dad sat me down to have 'the talk'. Back then, I'd humored him, and noted that he wouldn't have gone there if he didn't have his suspicions. By the time he was my age, he and my mom were already pregnant with me. I guess since I knew he was in no position to preach abstinence to me given the circumstances that he'd suck it up and leave us to do what teenagers do. I didn't think he'd be happy about it. But backpedaling with me and intimidating Reed? I hadn't expected that.

"So what do I do?" I sigh.

"Look. He's never going to give you his blessing. But he's feeling insecure. I think he just wants proof that you respect him—and yourself—enough to give yourself to someone who deserves to have you. He knows he can't stop you. But he wants to be sure that nothing is clouding your judgment. Show him you're mature enough to decide. Trust me, he'll back off."

Chapter Nine

The Final Rule

Reed

I don't like to hover, but hovering is exactly what I'm doing. My father is in his study, reading with the door open, and I've casually strolled by three times. The first time was to grab a glass of water from the kitchen, the second to take it back to my room. When I passed a third time to grab a DVD from the living room, I thought I saw him look up from his book as I passed. Now I'm standing, out of sight, outside the door, grasping to think of an overture when his voice breaks through.

"I can bring you a chair if you plan to stay out there

all night."

Alright. I'm embarrassed, but not too embarrassed to feign innocence or make an excuse. I stroll in tentatively.

"Good book?" I ask lamely.

He removes his glasses long enough to rub his eyes. "I could take a break."

He stands then, stretching a little, and moves to the entrance to close the door. Instead of making his way to the liquor trolley, to pour us something to drink, he places his hands in his pockets and continues to look at me.

"Things with Aubrey are still going well?"

I'm a strange mixture of pride and trepidation. Because they are going well. So well that I feel us hurdling closer to the main event.

"Your lessons have been…invaluable," I say earnestly, hoping that gratitude is evident by my tone. "I've been practicing everything you taught me. I won't say I've mastered any of it, but I'm getting better," I finish humbly.

His own eyes hold the now-familiar pride along with a deep warmth that reminds me how much I love my dad. "I'm glad, son."

But we both know this isn't what I've come to say.

"I think we're close," I say, not quite knowing where I'm going with it but having to say it all the same. "And I was wondering whether there's more…instruction."

Hands still in his pockets, he nods in subtle understanding.

"We've gone over all the technicalities…" my father

murmurs. And he's right. We've talked—in detail—about full-out penetration sex. "And even some of the finer points," he mentions gently.

But I still don't feel ready. I know for sure that I've got more game than nearly any other kid at my school—my dad was right about the locker room talk, and about the porn. It's so theatrical, I can barely watch it anymore. Yet, no matter how much wiser I've become, I still feel green.

"I know...I just feel like..." I hesitate. I don't want to say it out loud. "I mean...at this point, the bar's pretty high. She knows how I'm capable of making her feel...doing other things..."

My father listens patiently as I run my fingers through my hair and look at the fire.

"I think she's expecting some grand finale—some even bigger payoff once we go all the way. But I know I won't last. I know it'll be a big disappointment."

When I look back at him, his eyes are on me, but there's a kind of faraway look in his eyes—the kind that shows me he's choosing his words very carefully. I prepare myself, then— for him to let me down easy when he confirms my biggest fear. Instead, he says something completely unexpected.

"I don't know whether you and Aubrey will end up together," he begins, and I'm stunned into silence. "I know she's your first love, and that first love feels eternal, but that's the nature of it. When you're in it, it always does."

He's looking at me intensely, the half of his face that is turned in the direction of the fire is illuminated in soft yellows and oranges, and all of a sudden, the scene seems surreal. And I know that what he's about to tell me is more important than anything he's said in the weeks before.

"This is a defining moment in her life—and I'm not talking about the moment that scares you. I'm talking about all the moments you've spent—and will spend—loving her. Your job isn't to be the best sex she's ever had. It's to show her to expect nothing less from any man than the utmost respect, utter selflessness, and pure devotion. Your job with Aubrey—and any other woman you find yourself with down the road—is to leave her better than you found her. That's the bigger picture, Reed. That's the final rule."

And, in that moment, when it all comes together, it hits me with force. All this time, I thought I was learning how to be a rock star in bed. But, there's always been a higher purpose. I love Aubrey. So much that I don't want her to ever settle for someone too lazy to worship her body like the temple it is. I may not be the best she ever has, but I want to set the standard—to show her at least how a woman deserves to be treated. I want her to know that the boy who she gave all of her firsts to held them like the treasured gifts they are.

My father seems to sense that I'm too emotional to speak. Laying a gentle hand on my shoulder, he leads me to the door. With every slow step, I struggle for words to thank him. Talking about these things has opened up brand new territory for us, and it's meant more to me than he knows. I feel compelled to say something now. With the final rule has come the last lesson, and part of me feels as if a door is closing.

"I'll never forget this," I say as we draw nearer to the door.

I half-expect him to make light of my gratitude—to tell me that I'd better not forget anything if I'm to pass it on to my own son years from now. But when I turn toward him, I'm surprised to see that his own eyes are shining.

"Do you know my greatest wish for you?" he asks, and I can hear the emotion in his voice. "It's not for you to become a Whitney. I know what it's like…to have big shoes to fill…to feel the weight of the world's expectations."

Now it's my eyes that are shining, because I do feel that weight—have felt it all my life.

"Since the day I first held you in my arms, Reed…all I have ever wanted was for you to become a decent person, who values kindness and compassion over accomplishments and material things. I am never prouder of you than I am in the moments when I see how lovingly you treat Aubrey."

We hug, then, for a long time, and I feel like a little boy. I think of the photo on the mantlepiece, of him smiling at the camera and holding me the day I come home from the hospital. I think of his hand on my shoulder as I sobbed when we buried my pet goldfish in the backyard when I was six. I think of him taking me for ice cream the day of my first piano recital when I froze on stage and I couldn't perform. I think about how, for all of his regal formality at times, he's always been right here with me.

We both sniff a little as we pull away, and as I open the door, he gives me a final pat on the back. I can feel him watching me from the door as I reach the bottom of the stairs.

"Reed," he calls quietly, and when I look back at him, I see the hint of a smile on his face. "Next Friday...we're seeing a show in the city, and we got a hotel. We're taking Nikki and her friend."

"Oh," I say, surprised. It's a non-sequitur. "What are you seeing?"

His smile becomes more than a hint.

"Reed...", he repeats with emphasis. "We're seeing a show in the city, and we got a hotel."

Oh.

"No wild parties, okay? But if you want *company*," he says with meaning. "It's fine if you invite a friend."

Holy shit.

Five minutes later, I'm texting Aubrey.

What are you doing Friday night?

Chapter Ten

The Range

Aubrey

"What are you up to today?" I ask my dad a minute after I come downstairs on Saturday morning and find him at the kitchen table. I've grabbed a box of Cinnamon Toast Crunch from the cabinet and am about to drown it in what looks like the last of the milk. He's got his coffee in one hand, paper in the other, and his reading glasses are halfway down his nose. He mumbled a 'good morning' when I walked in, but now he looks up.

"Haven't decided yet." He says it so elusively that I know

he's skeptical of my motives in asking. He thinks I'm pressing into his schedule to find out when he'll be out of the house.

"We haven't been to the range in awhile…" I trail off a second before I take my first bite. "I thought maybe we'd shoot a few dozen rounds."

He closes his paper and folds it neatly on the table. "Yeah. That'd be nice." When he looks surprised that I'm asking because I want to spend time with him, and not ask whether I can do something with Reed, I feel a little guilty.

An hour later, we're at the private practice range that's only open to law enforcement. It's owned by the county, so we had to drive a ways to get there. He indulges me in the car by letting me plug in my play list. I know he doesn't always love my music, but when a Taylor Swift song he likes comes on, he smiles and asks me to turn it up.

I'm too young to own my gun, but the Ruger 22 semi-automatic pistol I shoot with is one he bought for me. I've been an almost perfect shot since I was around twelve. It takes me less than thirty seconds to get through the first magazine. It was a total of ten rounds, but when the target zips back up to me on the line, it has only four holes because I've shot through each of them at least twice. Three each in the center of the forehead, two in each eye, and the final three through the heart.

"You're better than me," he observes with pride. "Took me years to even hold a candle to what you can do. I think you might be ready for a nine."

"A nine, huh?" I quip. "I was thinking my next one

would be a three-fifty-seven." I pull an earplug out of one ear.

"Oh, you were, were you?" He's smiling now, too.

I just shrug. "I learned from the best."

"Guess you're right about that…" he softens a bit at the compliment. And I know that, even though we just got here, now is my chance.

"I'll miss this when I leave for college," I say more quietly, taking the other bud out of my ear. I watch him do the same. "But I know that, when I'm out there on my own, you've given me everything I need to be okay."

We're alone at the range. No one else's shots to distract us. No one else to witness, or tarnish, this moment. Sensing that I have something on my chest, he places his pistol on the counter and removes his glasses.

"You know I'll be responsible, right?"

And because he's not stupid, he knows what I'm talking about.

"Remember what you told me the day I got my purple belt?" I ask softly. I couldn't have been older than eight. "I cracked a joke after the belt ceremony. Told you that since I'd mastered my roundhouse kick, no one could ever mess with me again. You told me the kick had nothing to do with it— that I'd already made that statement true the second I fully comprehended the most important lesson in martial arts— to never give away my power."

He's silent for so long that I think to put my ears back in, and keep on shooting. I've said what I came to say, and he's heard it. Besides, he's never been one for excesses of sentimentality.

"I was seventeen when you were born." His words halt my action. "Should've scared the living shit out of me. No high school degree. No job. Never changed a diaper or warmed up a bottle of milk. But the first time I held you— apart from the joy—I was just…ready. I could taste the sweat I would pour into giving you your best life."

I feel a lump form in my throat.

"What I didn't know then was how little credit I would deserve for turning you into the person you've become. Even as a baby, you were fierce—and determined. You've always known your own power. At some point, I realized my job wasn't to make you strong. It was to teach you how to make good choices. Surround yourself with good people. Stay rooted to what matters."

I somehow find my voice. "And?"

I see his verdict in his eyes before he speaks it aloud. "You don't need me to choose for you anymore, Aubs. I know I don't always act like I know it, but I do. You're a woman now."

And, in that moment, I don't care that the tears have started to fall. I don't care that my heart has heavied with mourning. I don't dwell on the paradoxical reality that lead- ing my father to exactly the conclusion I wanted him to draw has filled me with a sense of loss. I'm suddenly nostalgic for the days when I was small enough to sit on his shoulders, for the dozens of dress-up tea parties he enthusiastically attended. I think of all the times he let me push the siren button in the cruiser, just because it made me happy, and laughed with me while I giggled like a tiny maniac. I had set all of this up to help him let me go. But now it's me who wants to hold on. And when I launch myself into his arms, I do. I hold on to him for a long time.

Chapter Eleven

The Drill

Reed

Fuck.

I'm so busy feeling dejected while toweling off my hair that I barely notice my father standing a few steps inside my door. Embarrassment prevails as I watch his gaze triangulate among the open box of condoms on my nightstand, my trash can full of failures, and my face.

"Couldn't wait?" Both of his eyebrows are raised.

I hasten to stride over to the nightstand and pluck the half-empty box of condoms off of display, opening the drawer and shoving them as far back as they will go. The unused condoms, which I threw toward the trash can in haphazard frustration, are littered in its vicinity. I push the two that hang over the rim all the way inside. As I do all of this, I make sure to keep one hand on the towel around my waist. Because the only thing that could make this moment more embarrassing would be for my towel to fall off.

"It's not what you think," I mutter, thankful that it wasn't my mother or Nikki who walked in on this scene. I'd spent the better part of the last hour practicing how to put on a condom. Forty five minutes of the hour before that had been spent driving to Middletown to by the offending latex items from the far more anonymous CVS. Paying for them at the counter would have been embarrassing enough. I didn't want to buy them from old Mr. Parvin at the only pharmacy in our town.

If I'd been worried about being overexcited when Aubrey and I finally did the deed, I have little to worry about now. Because nothing had killed my erections faster than trying to roll on those evil contraptions. I'd bought a box of twelve, figuring I'd practice with one or two and be ready for the big night. My little practice exercise had run me through half a box, and despite my efforts, I'd mastered nothing.

"I was practicing," I say, not meeting my father's eyes as I grab a t-shirt and boxers from my drawer and slip back into my bathroom. As I drop my towel and dress myself quickly, I hear him open the drawer. When I emerge he is, as expected, studying the pack of Trojans I'd replaced just seconds before.

"Well, I've found your problem," he says. "You bought the wrong kind."

The trip back to Middletown, disguised as a dinner run, is barely noticed by Nikki or my mom. I can't help sulking a bit on the ride over. However confident I am that my father will reveal the solution to my problem, I am humiliated. I'd felt so proud of myself to have come up with the idea of one more thing I could do to make Friday night go more smoothly. My failure reminds me of what an amateur I still am.

"Magnums," my father says definitively, breaking the silence we'd shared since we left home. We are staring at the same astonishingly large wall I'd been puzzled by not so long before. I'd stayed away from the ones that looked a bit too adventurous—vibrating rings and flavors are something I don't think I'll ever want to work my way up to. I remember having seen the box he's referring to, but I thought they were just another brand. So I pick up a box of twelve, scrutinizing the package so I can figure out what makes these different. And then I see it: *Large size condoms*, reads the caption below the bold print, in unhelpfully understated text.

"They were too small?" I stammer.

My father smirks over at me. "Way too small," he says with satisfaction. "Don't be embarrassed," he murmurs as he plucks a larger box off the display and hands it to me, replacing my smaller one. Before walking away, presumably to have me fly solo at the checkout counter, he's still smirking when he says, "It's a good problem to have."

Aubrey

I'm on the sofa pretending to read a book when my father comes downstairs in full camping gear. His backpack, rods, and tackle box are already sitting by the door. It seems all the weekends he's spent neglecting his bromance with Paul, his best friend of more than thirty years, have finally caught up to him. He's knocked off early from work so that the and Paul can make it up to that spot they like before nightfall.

"You got the money I left you for groceries?" he asks.

I put down my book and give him a nod.

"And you programmed Rita's number into your phone?"

"I double-checked when I got home from school," I say, standing in preparation to say goodbye.

"Good," he nods a bit absently, looking me over for a long moment instead of making his way toward the door. "I guess I'm ready, then." But he still doesn't move.

I think it's a relief to both of us, this new normal we've discovered. Since that morning at the range, there's been a shift. He never came out and said the rules were changing, but a sort of don't ask, don't tell dynamic has emerged. Instead of grilling me about where I'm going, who I'll be with, and reminding me for the umpteenth time that 9:30 is curfew, his language has completely changed. My jaw had nearly dropped when, on that very same evening, he'd thrown out that I should text him if I'd be out later than midnight.

It didn't end there. All week, he'd given me more keys to my own freedom. We'd gone to the bank one day after school and he'd taken his name off of the savings account he'd been a custodian on since I was born. We'd talked to a financial planner about how much I should save, spend, and invest. I know he's only still standing there because breaking the habit of digging for all the details is unfamiliar, but not unwelcome. I get the sense that he's found freedom in this, too. He hasn't set down any guidelines for what I can or can't do this weekend. And I know he won't ask.

"Love you, dad," I say, standing on my toes to kiss him on the cheek as I give him a hug. Both of us hold on a little longer than we would have seven days before.

"Love you too, Aubs."

And then he's gone. And some part of me realizes that at this very same moment, Reed's parents and sister are on the same road headed out of town. When my mind's reflections finally kick my body into action, I head up to the shower. I've got a little grooming to do.

Chapter Twelve

Fumbling Towards Ecstasy

Reed

Playing the piano usually relaxes me, but as I stare at the ivory keys, I can't bring myself to touch a single one. No song fits this occasion. No melody will calm my nerves. No distraction will keep me from looking at my watch every forty-five seconds. It was a stupid plan anyway. The volume of the music will prevent me from hearing her car in the driveway, from knowing the exact second she arrives.

Sitting on my bench, with anxiety instead of calm, makes the piano itself feel foreign to me—as if it isn't even mine. This is akin to what it feels like those first moments when I sit at an unfamiliar piano on an unfamiliar stage, sensing critical eyes and expectant ears on me, the anonymous crowd hungry for a perfect performance. I've been here before.

The only way out is through it.

This time, it's my mother's wisdom that infiltrates my mind. In this situation, there is only one decision to make. Do or die. Fight or flight. Show up or don't. And if you opt to do, or fight, or show up, the only thing to do is to start playing—to trust that all the practice you've put in will pay off.

For a fleeting moment, I wish that this could have happened for Aubrey and me the same way it does for other teenagers: fumbling towards ecstasy in the back seat of a car or in a locked bedroom at a party. A little liquid courage, the imminence of curfew speeding things along…add in premature ejaculation, and—boom—it's over.

But when I do hear Aubrey's car, and make my way on shaky legs to the door, what I see when I open it forces me to perish the thought. The second I lay eyes on her, I know the memories I want of this night aren't drunken moments or foggy windows in humid cars. I want to remember her shy smile and the clean, woodsy scent of her perfume. I want it to be in the privacy of my own room. And I want us to have all night.

"I warmed up the jacuzzi," I offer, after I've taken her bag and ushered her inside. I've thought this part through. It would be entirely too awkward to go straight up to my room.

"I didn't bring my bathing suit," she apologizes, though

her voice is laced with relief.

My smile defies the thundering of my heart.

"Then it's a good thing we have the place to ourselves."

I make an event out of undressing her in the sun room off of the deck. I've been looking forward to this part. She's wearing a top I've never seen before—a dark blue fitted shirt that hugs her in all the right places, and a pair of jeans she knows I love. The dark blue bra and french cut panties I find underneath them also look new. Telling her how beautiful she is to me feels more right than anything else I've done all day. Watching her entire body blush beneath me as I reverently remove her bra, and then her panties, elicits a silent prayer of thanks to whatever gods are listening. I am blessed to have this night, this woman, as my first.

We're only in the cold air for a few seconds on the short walk from the back door to the hot tub before we ease into the hot water. We sit silently at first, holding hands as we watch the sun set over the mountains in the distance. My mind is everywhere I thought it wouldn't be. I think of how many nights I spent in my room playing video games instead of enjoying this. How much I'll miss it when we leave for college. How a fateful coin toss will decide whether first dibs on this house will be Nikki's or mine.

I hope first dibs come to me. I want to live here again one day. I want Aubrey to live here with me. I want a jungle gym for our children to play in on one of the open expanses of lawn. I know it's a strange thing for someone so young to want. But, even before Aubrey, I've known I was meant for this. This place is, and always will be, my one true home. Could this place ever be as magical to her as it is to me? When I look down at Aubrey, studying her face for clues, her impish smile covers underlying emotions of amusement and joy. And I know the next serious talk I have with my father will involve my grandmother's engagement ring.

But there's no time for that now. I'm looking down at her and she's looking up at me, and I need only an inch or three to seal this moment with a kiss. I think of our first date, and our first kiss and our first 'I love you'. I think of piano recitals and duck ponds and expensive spirits consumed in front of roaring fires. I think of the thirty-five Magnums sitting upstairs in my drawer. I think of how thinking about all of these things is turning my semi into something more significant. And my plans to ease into this fly out the window the moment I feel the eagerness of her tongue as it presses in to tangle with mine the moment our lips touch.

Things escalate quickly. We go from kissing shoulder-to-shoulder to kissing with her tucked under my one arm, to my erection stalking her hot, slippery center like a cruise-guided missile when she maneuvers to sit side-saddle on my lap. We'd been submerged to our shoulders, but her new position has placed her breasts just above the water line. When she arches her back at some point instead of returning her lips to mine, I know what she wants. So I lower my mouth to her beautifully puckered nipple, which may only be so hard and pebbled as a result of the cold, but, holy shit, it turns me on.

This is the first time we've both been completely naked—skin to skin—and beyond each of us writhing and rubbing down below to create more friction, the coolness of the night air against my warm skin and the motion of the spinning jets feels sublime.

We breathe heavily in-between kisses, as if we've actually been underwater. I'm sucking one nipple and fondling the other and she's grinding so deliciously below that I move the hand that's doing the fondling beneath the water, knowing I can do her one better. When my thumb finds her clit and my middle finger finds her opening, we both moan and her nipple makes a wet popping sound as she lifts my chin to recapture my lips with hers. I slide my long finger in, massaging her just the way she likes it, but she's working me as much as I'm working her.

When she becomes too breathless to kiss, her hand grips the back of my neck and she arches back once more. I feel her pussy coil even tighter around me as my mouth lavishes attention on her other nipple. I am rock fucking hard and my other hand holds her waist to better-allow my hips to mimic my finger's rhythm. My cock is right there, closer than he's ever been to heaven.

"It's like you're fucking me," she says in a lust-filled voice I've never heard.

And the small part of my brain that isn't preoccupied with these astounding new sensations, pieces something together. I'm beyond thinking. Beyond planning. Beyond worrying about what I should do. The only thing in the world that is important right now is making us feel good, and my body is so sure of what it wants that instinct is taking over.

"Is that what you want, baby?" I practically growl as I interrupt my own rhythm to give more attention to her g-spot.

Holy hell. Who are you and what have you done with the real Reed?

And, for a disorienting moment, I honestly don't know. Because suddenly, I'm hellbent on hurtling her toward a legendary orgasm. Abruptly, I have a deep need for her to tell me how badly she wants my cock. I'm already having visions of what I'll do when she does come—how the second I take my fingers out, I'll slide my dick in. I think of the thirty-five condoms upstairs and the zero condoms down here. I think of my vow not to hurt her, to take it slowly enough to let her adjust to my size. But in this moment, I want things I've never wanted. Feel things I've never felt. I've never felt so out of control with her.

"I want it so bad," she moans. "It's not even fair." Her voice is the perfect balance between utter pleasure and sheer pain.

Her words satisfy me so deeply, her body tangles with mine so magically, that I'm pretty sure I'm about to let go of my grip and surrender. The beast has awakened. It's not some horny monster. It's some authentic—maybe the most authentic—part of me. This is his domain. He doesn't want to share it with sweet, sensitive, desperately-in-love Reed. This was what my father had warned me about that very first day. And I'm dangerously close to breaking Rule Number One.

Aubrey

Yes.

It's one of only two coherent thoughts I can form in my mind. Though, I'm absently aware that I've turned into a wanton hussy. I'm spewing off incoherent thoughts to Reed, but my mind can barely fathom what's being said. Because all I can think right now is, *yes*. And, *more*.

I must voice this aloud, because at some point, Reed trades one finger for two. The way this stretches me shows me the definition of what it means for something to hurt so good. I'm not afraid of his cock anymore. God, I want it. I think I say so. And right after I do, I come spectacularly on his fingers.

I lose myself for a minute, and when I come to and open my eyes to him, he looks wild. I don't know what possesses me to shift my body again, straddling him this time, my knees on the underwater bench, my hips pivoting as my overexcited center searches for his cock. Coming felt amazing, but I'm still so aroused. Maybe if we just keep going, I can come again. I reach down to rub his tip against my entrance, but his firm grip touches my arm.

"Condom," he says firmly.

My inner hussy instructs me to tell him that, as a back-up, I went on the pill. But what little sense I have left knows he's right.

He helps me out of the hot tub. I feel a little woozy when I stand. I don't know whether it's because of the orgasm or because we've been in there too long. He leads me inside and begins to dry me off with a huge towel, mumbling something about how we shouldn't be dripping if we don't want to slip on the marble floor. I can't stop ogling him. He is complete-ly naked, and so hard that his cock stands so far upright, I half expect it to bounce against his abs. After we're dry, we're hurrying through his enormous mansion, walking quickly but cautiously over the marble floor, and breaking into a run when we hit the carpeted stairs. When we get to his bedroom, I practically jump on the bed. He walks to his bedside table and pulls out the largest box of condoms I have ever seen.

"I'll explain later."

I wait only until he's pulled a single foil packet off of the strip before I coax him back to me. It's been a few minutes since we left the Jacuzzi, but I'm still hot as hell. I'm ready to pick up right where we left off.

He's hard against my leg and I'm already rutting against him again.

"Please," I say between kisses. "I don't want to wait."

But, for as natural, and easy, as our little display down-stairs was, the hesitation I know so well returns to his face.

"I don't want to lose control." He looks down into my eyes. "And I think I almost did."

"I liked it."

He shakes his head.

"Down there…you have no idea how close I was to fucking you."

"But you didn't," I point out. "You took care of me. You got us here. And now we're going to do it right."

Something in his eyes changes. He kisses me deeply one more time, before rising to his knees and putting on the condom. And it's all happening so fast. His tip at my entrance. The first few inches he pushes in. The pain followed by the pleasure.

"Fuuuuccckk…." He says. He's out of breath, even though he's not moving. I don't think he's all the way in, but I love the way he feels inside me. I can feel everything—can feel him throbbing every few seconds, can feel how hard he is, can feel his amazing girth. It is my new favorite feeling. The very best in the world.

Reed

"Fuuuuccckk…." I say.

Technically, it's everything I've been led to believe it will be. Hot. Tight. Slippery wet. The heaviness of my balls. But it's so much more than that. It's seeing stars every time she coils more tightly around me. It's lightning bolts every time her pussy twitches. It's the tingling that starts in my back, building toward an orgasm that I can already tell will be different from any I've ever felt before.

But, most of all, it's wanting to move. Because as amazing as this feels, it's not enough. And moving will make it so much better. I want to close my eyes and piston my hips. I want to drive into her until I can feel her entrance on my balls. But I don't want either of those things more than I want her to enjoy this.

And, fuck, I can see that she does. And that's a turn-on all on its own. My movements are slow, and only about half of me is inside of her, but her body, and her words, are confirming that she likes this. Every word of praise brings me closer. Every rise of her hips to meet me eggs me on. I'm going slowly, but even with that, it feels too good. We've only been at it for a minute, but I know I'm going to come.

"I want you to come, baby," she says. And that spurs me forward most of all. Before the words leave her mouth, I'm emptying inside her. I think I'm spewing gibberish, because intelligent speech is one of the many faculties I've lost control of, and, *holy fuck,* is it hard to sound dignified in the middle of an orgasm as spectacular as this.

That next moment—the one in which I'm supposed to carefully remove the condom, gaze down lovingly at Aubrey, and utter profound words that are the perfect coda to our lovemaking—never comes. I'm out of breath and on my back, staring dazedly at my ceiling. My arm is slung across my forehead and the uncomfortable sensation of the forgotten condom and oozing semen are more than I can worry about right now. When I do turn my head to give Aubrey the best loving look I can muster, I can't. Because we're both grinning like idiots.

Grinning turns to giggling. Giggling turns to peals of laughter. When we begin to punctuate our hilarity with kisses, bad puns, and crass euphemisms for what we just did, only Aubrey's threat to pee the bed if we don't stop is enough to calm us down.

"Did you at least come?" I ask, thinking I know the answer but not completely sure. If a U.F.O. had landed on my bed during those last moments, I don't think I would have noticed.

"No. But *you* did," she smirks.

I turn a bit serious as I throw her a repentant look and speak an earnest vow. "I'll get better at this."

"Are you kidding?" She scoffs. "We already rock." And her kind gesture of buoying my injured pride only makes me love her more.

"Wanna head back down to the jacuzzi? Grab something to eat on the way down? Maybe look at the stars?" I ask, settling her into the crook of my shoulder and kissing her forehead.

"Mmm-hmmm", she hums. "But maybe you should clean up, or take a shower or something first."

I not-so-discreetly sniff in the direction of my armpits. This causes her to roll her eyes.

She points downward. "You have a gold wrapper stuck to your ass and a condom hanging off of your dick."

Chapter Thirteen

Epilogue

Reed

"I miss these," Dad says as he helps himself to another half of a grilled cheese sandwich. I've perfected my recipe over the years. Sourdough bread, sharp white cheddar, Irish butter...sometimes I even do grilled cheese and bacon, and I fry the sandwich in bacon grease. On my father's request for this rare father/son lunch, today is one of those days.

"Mom still got you on a diet?" I ask needlessly. I already know the answer. Since he had to get a stent put in one of his arteries because of a blockage three years ago, she's had him on a leash.

"Have you ever been forced to eat a sandwich made with Vegenaise?" he asks with thinly-veiled disgust.

The look on my face mirrors his. "No. That sounds atrocious."

"Believe me—it is. Why do you think I arranged a spa day for your mother and the girls? I was starving for a decent lunch."

He looks at me gratefully as I hand him a beer and I sit at the kitchen counter to join him. We just remodeled and he seems to approve. It's one of many changes we've made over the years. It still strikes me as strange, though, living here without my parents. It's been my home all my life, with the exception of the years we spent in college and grad school. I always knew that, one day, my parents would pass it on to one of us. We've taken over the main house and they live in the guest house on the border of our forest whenever they come and visit. But they spend the majority of their retirement traveling the world and relaxing in their home on Maui.

And when I say "relaxing", that's not what I mean at all. Even at seventy-five they still bump like rabbits. We had to give them a stern talking-to and have a Do Not Disturb sign made for the guest cottage door. When our kids got old enough to start wandering down for innocent visits to Mom-Mom and Pop-Pop and had a few close calls, that was a sure sign we needed a system. There may have also been a skinny dipping incident in the swimming hole. But I don't like to talk about that.

The kids are older now. Aubrey, like my own mother, had so many fertility problems that we did IVF and ended up with Norah and Sedona. Nathan was a surprise who came less than a year later. There were days when we thought we'd never survive the early years—three small children in diapers had been a challenge—but now that they're teenagers, I sometimes miss the baby days.

But this—what I'm about to do today—is something I've been looking forward to for years. Unbeknownst to Nate, today is the day he'll learn about The Rules. I wipe my hands and rise from my seat to grab a paper shopping bag I've placed discreetly out of sight. It carries the name of a high-end papery in the city. I went there yesterday morning to pick up the book, and the afternoon locked in my study, transcribing. I hand my father the handmade leather journal, placing next to it the exquisite matching box that secures it with lock and key. I think he knows what it is before he opens it. Yet, confirmation brings a smile.

"You *remembered* all of this?"

"Are you kidding? I wrote it down. It was a lot of information." I watch with satisfaction as he pages through the book, his youthful eyes sparkling brightly as nostalgia writes itself on his face. "Fond memories, huh?" I murmur.

"Fond memories, indeed."

"Nate is ready." Another thing he's probably already figured out. "This afternoon, I'll invite him into the study. So don't be surprised if he can't look you and mom in the eye tomorrow."

"Noted." He chuckles at that.

"Any pointers?" I ask. Because even though he may not get around as well as he used to, and he's not stronger than me anymore...even though my dad has reached an age where he needs my help more than I need his, he's never stopped being my greatest supporter, or giving the best advice.

"Have fun with it." My dad is still smiling. "You know what teenagers are like. They think they know everything. They think you were never young, or cool. They like to pretend they came about from immaculate conception. Knock him down a notch or two. Show him his old dad can teach him a few things."

Now I'm smiling, too. "Alright."

"And throw him some zingers," he continues a second later. "Tell him a few things that he thinks will scar him for life. Messing with him is all part of the fun."

Now we're both laughing. We raise our beers in silent toast and each take a drink.

Nate

"Hey, Pop-Pop, hey Dad," I say, strolling into the kitchen, where I find my dad and my grandfather laughing together over a couple of beers. Mom-Mom must be out somewhere. Everyone knows she hardly lets him drink. Everyone also knows that he comes up to the main house to raid our kitchen the second she goes out. Last week, before she took my sisters shopping, she warned me to hide the pan of butterscotch bars if Pop-Pop had more than three.

"Nathan, my boy!" I think Pop-Pop may be a little drunk. I'll bet your tolerance really suffers when you're hardly allowed to touch the stuff. But his handshake is firm, and his pat on my back has a kick to it. For a septuagenarian, my grandpa's pretty cool.

Dad and Pop-Pop are close, which has never surprised me. Growing up, my dad was, like, the perfect kid. He never drank or did drugs, he got good grades, had mom home before curfew, and never broke a single rule. Aunt Nikki was the black sheep—the rule-breaker, and rabble-rouser. The adventurous one who was never afraid to take risks and make mistakes. I'm more like Aunt Nikki. The twins are more like dad. I respect the hell out of him, but the older I get, the less I think we have in common.

It's Saturday. I just spent all morning with my girlfriend, Leslie. We were "checking out the new exhibit" at the modern art museum for a school project. At least that's what I told my parents. I don't feel good about kinda sorta lying to them about my whereabouts, but it keeps them off my back. Besides, what am I supposed to say to them? That research for our school assignment only took one of the past four hours? That the museum didn't even open until ten even though I left the house at eight? That my early departure allowed for two solid hours of serious make-out time?

My mom and dad would laugh me out of the house if I told them how serious I am about Leslie. *Serious about Leslie?* I can practically hear my mother say. *You'd better get serious about cleaning that room.* I can imagine how my dad would chime in then, looking at me from above his bifocals and laying into his own lecture. *And you'd better get serious about finding a job for the summer. This isn't a hotel.*

When Pop-Pop leaves abruptly, chugging the half a bottle of beer that remains like a frat boy, before he heads down to the cottage, and my dad suggests I join him in his study, I'm immediately suspicious. I scour my brain—not so much for things I might have done wrong, because that list is too long—but for things I have more than a snowball's chance in hell of getting caught for.

I can think of only two recent candidates. Last Wednesday, I forged dad's signature on a note to get me out of the last two periods of class. If questioned about this, I'll tell the truth (that I was with Leslie) and mention in my defense that the last two periods were only gym and study hall. Apart from that, I was the mastermind behind humiliating this kid who's been grabbing girls asses and tits. I put invisible anti-theft powder on his locker and his car door so that he'd have bright red pigment on the palms of is hands for a couple of days. Then I started a viral text thread that showed a pair of red handprints and huge lettering that said "Hands off of what's not yours." The school wasn't doing shit about it. If my dad gave me guff, I'd tell him the guy had it coming. I'd see how he liked knowing that two of this asshole's victims were the twins.

"Scotch?" my dad asks, closing the door before striding to his liquor trolley.

"Thank you," I accept. Because I'm sixteen and if he's offering me a drink at one o'clock in the afternoon, I'm betting there's something going on.

"You and Leslie are close," he begins after a few minutes.

Hmmm…he wants to talk about Leslie.

"Your mother seems to think you two are—being intimate—with each other."

"You and mom talk about my sex life?"

"Suppose we do. Would we find there's much to talk about?"

This feels like a trick. He's trying to get me to admit something without telling me why I'm here.

"I guess that depends on your definition of sex," I say cooly, getting ready to sling some new age shit at him. "Earlier generations defined sex as intercourse, but I prefer not to limit my concept of sex to penetration."

"So, by your own definition, are you sexually active?"

I don't let him see that my own misdirection has led me to a set of questions that it shames me to explore. Leslie and I have fooled around, but it's never led to a mutual climax. Which means that for all the hours we spend kissing and fondling, they haven't culminated in much.

"What's this all about, dad? Is it about birth control? STDs? I know how to protect myself against all that stuff."

"It's not about any of that," he says, giving nothing more away.

"Does mom not like Leslie?"

"Your mother thinks Leslie is charming."

"Then what is this about?"

He swirls the large ice cube in his glass before fixing his eyes back upon me.

"An inheritance you never knew you had coming. One that you would gladly trade for your financial inheritance if you had the wisdom of age to look back and make a choice."

He leans forward in his chair, then, giving me as serious a look as I've ever seen from him. Eyes that are identical to mine hold something unexpected, and deep.

"You are a Whitney, and were therefore born with certain natural—*endowments*—that predispose you to success with women. But, there is a beauty in sex which, if you could only grow to appreciate it—an art which, if you could only commit to learning it—will bring you and the women in your life such divine fulfillment as most mortals never know. It is wisdom that my father passed down to me and that his father passed down to him and that you will pass to your own sons when it is time. It is the art of worship,Nate, and it has very little to do with sex."

Author's Notes

Thank you for reading *The Art of Worship*! I have never had as much fun with characters as I've had with Preston and Reed. Writing them made me want to organize a crack team of parents dedicated to saving the world from bad sex, one teenager at a time. My boys are still little, but I'm already working on Mr. Blades to start the family tradition. As a mother, I take seriously my responsibility to raise boys who don't leave the toilet seat up, who truly understand the meaning of consent, and who don't subscribe to the porn version of sex. After all, I want someone to marry them one day…

Though the sex talks I got from my parents were very different from those given by Preston and Kate, writing The Art of Worship recalled fond memories. Many other elements of my story were similar to Aubrey and Reed's. I lost my v-card when I was in high school, to my very first boyfriend. It was everything young love should be and we dated for a long time. We met at Sunday School (LOL!) and there were plenty of shenanigans when it came to sneaking around.

If you liked (or hated!) *The Art of Worship*, I would appreciate hearing your thoughts in a review. I always love hearing from readers, and reviews are a huge help to indie authors like me. My next novel, *The Secret Ingredient*, is about a well-loved television chef who takes a summer rental in an idyllic seaside town to write her next cookbook. When she finds out that her neighbor—a sexy plastic surgeon who's on break from his tour abroad—likes to dabble in the kitchen, she asks him to be her assistant. *The Secret Ingredient* will be a very special release. I can't share the details yet, but if you want to be among the first to know the score, head to my web site and sign up to receive news about this release. And if you want a sneak peek, a preview begins on the next page.

Want to ask me about my books or just say hello? E-mail me at kilby@kilbyblades.com!

Sneak Peek of *The Secret Ingredient*

It was a delicious sleep, the kind that could only be achieved when the day was settling and the breeze swirled a mix of warmth from the sun and coolness from the sea. The hammock upon which Max lazily napped swung gently with his weight, the pages of his forgotten book stirring with the wind. He had missed this tremendously, his cozy home on the water, but work kept him away. But now he had a month—four glorious weeks!—to unwind and enjoy his peaceful home.

It was Cujo's faraway bark that roused him—far away, not as in faint through the haze of Max's dream—far away, as in no longer in the vicinity of his master. He woke himself more fully as he realized that his dog must have wandered off of his land. When not terrorizing sand crabs or chasing gophers through their holes, the feisty beagle liked helping himself to the vegetables in Mrs. McGregor's garden.

Mrs. McGregor. Max did not relish the thought of knocking on her door, though if Cujo had misbehaved, presenting himself to apologize would be the only decent thing to do. There was nothing decent about Mrs. McGregor—not the revealing clothes she wore in Max's presence, and especially not her repeated propositions. The woman was married, a fact of which Max had reminded her many, many times. And he had no wish to run-in with her husband, Emmett, so he kept his distance whenever he could.

Slipping on his leather sandals, he placed his book on

the porch's edge, next to a half a bottle of beer that had long gone warm. He pocketed his sunglasses as he set his lips just so for a long, loud whistle for his dog. The houses here were far apart, though close enough that he might see Cujo's movement in the McGregor yard. He looked left, scanning the near corner of his neighbor's property line, surprised when a familiar answering bark came from the right.

He blinked in slight disbelief, not knowing how he hadn't seen it that morning. Lawn furniture and other signs of life now graced the adjoining yard. The house must have sold while he was away. His new neighbor had arrived.

The house next door had been vacant for quite some time. It was prime waterfront real estate, but with the economy what it was and many of the homeowners who bought in Longport using their properties as second homes, it was of little surprise that such a lovely (and expensive) house would sit awhile on the market.

Making his way down his back steps, he followed Cujo's bark, ducking through some hedges along the property line that afforded each home a bit of privacy. A woman whose face was obscured by a wide-brimmed sun hat and wavy brown hair sat sideways on a long pool chaise, facing his dog. She was scratching his scruff and serving him morsels from her own impressively-appointed plate. The little beagle's tail wagged happily behind him.

Cujo barked again, before relieving the woman of what looked like a succulent cube of beef. She looked up, but before Max could thank her for her grace in sharing her dinner with Cujo, he froze. The sheepish smile belonged to Marcella Dawes!

* * *

"Marcella's Bites" was more than a television show—it was Max's religion—and he worshipped at the altar of its host, chef extraordinaire and goddess of the kitchen Marcella Dawes. Though he traveled days at a time for work, he found solace from an emotionally taxing job through perfecting the art of cooking. He braised; he flambéd; he fricasseed. He paired his creations with fantastic wines. With him every step of the way was "Marcella's Bites". He found tremendous enjoyment in preparing the recipes from the show, and truly idolized its host.

Marcella was everything a woman should be—all confidence and curves and a true classic beauty to boot. He had often admired her generous proportions and everything that perfected them—those vibrant eyes, that gentle voice, and her mane of thick, dark hair. She was the type of woman whom he compared other women to, the kind of woman who spoiled a man from ever wanting to settle for less. The lady herself was as much a work of art as the confections she baked. She was exquisitely Rubenesque.

"In my defense, he's got some of the best puppydog eyes I've ever seen," she quipped somewhat nervously, a gorgeous blush staining her cheeks. "I hope you don't mind that I fed him."

Already, Max felt smitten.

"Cujo is shameless," he remarked finally, his voice edged

with wonder. "His begging left you with little choice."

She laughed, and it was music, its true melody amplified far beyond what could be heard on TV. It tickled him, prompting a sudden and genuine smile that felt fantastic to let show. Joking and lightness had little place in his everyday.

"Cujo? Really?"

She bit the corner of her lip to conceal what seemed like extreme mirth. The tiny gesture charmed him beyond reason.

"You didn't know him as a puppy," he murmured, fully taken with the beauty before him and astonished by how easily they'd begun to converse.

"Well, he seems like a sweet little thing now," she said, refocusing, for a moment, on petting him lovingly.

As her skilled fingers tousled the canine's fur, Max felt more than a little jealous.

"In any case, please let me know whether his begging ever becomes a bother," he recovered. "He enjoys food nearly as much as his master."

A brief silence fell upon them, though it was not altogether uncomfortable. She blushed slightly, but continued smiling, holding her gaze upon him as he greedily drank in her face. He marveled at her faint sprinkling of freckles, the way the sun lightened the ends of her hair, and the familiarity of her espresso eyes.

"I'm Max," he said finally, holding out what he hoped was a dry, steady hand. "And I'm sorry if I stared. I have seen you so often on television, as a celebrity, that it's somewhat strange to fathom that you've bought the house next door."

When she snorted, she even made that sound delightful.

"I'm hardly a celebrity!" she laughed. "And I'm just renting, actually. I'll have it for the rest of the summer."

She stood to greet him, returning his handshake with a soft but strong grip. She smelled of citrus and jasmine. The corner of her light-colored skirt billowed gently in the breeze, shifting against lickable calves. Max's indulgent eyes followed them upward, caressing her shapely thighs.

"Well, I really enjoy your show," he posited, hoping that sincerity, and not lust, colored his voice. Worse yet, he didn't want to come off like an obsessed fan boy—few things were more shameful than a thirty-five year old man sounding like a twelve year old girl with Bieber Fever.

"You cook?" she asked with what seemed like genuine interest.

"I dabble." he shrugged modestly.

"Outstanding" she nodded. "So I can count on you if I ever need to borrow a cup of sugar?"

Several critical organs stirred when her teeth closed down on a succulent bottom lip. Was it just wishful thinking, or could Marcella be flirting?

"My kitchen is at your disposal," he breathed.

The faint sound of a bell could be heard from the direction of their houses. She frowned a bit when it rang.

"Well, it's nice to meet you, Max. Sorry to cut it short, but I need to go check on my cake."

His disappointment was immediate. He did not want

her to leave.

"Marcella," he stated earnestly, "…the pleasure is mine."

She removed her hat and shook out her hair before fixing her eyes on him once again. Another delicious wave of her aroma crashed upon his wanting shores.

"You can call me Cella."

Acknowledgments

I dedicated this book to my treasured friend, Marcia. Not only was she an original beta reader for *The Art of Worship*, she's the personification of everything I love about writing, and this community. My ultimate dream is to get her writing again and to, one day, write an epically hilarious novel with her. My pro team was small on this one: Stacey, Elizabeth and Jada always make everything pretty. Britta and Jennifer promote the hell out of shit. Nicole, Liz, Rose and Leslie deal with my daily antics. Kisses, ladies!

About the Author

A high profile business executive by day, and a writer of smart contemporary fiction by night, Kilby earned her MBA from one of the nation's top business schools and currently serves as Chief Marketing Officer for a celebrated start-up. She juggles a busy business career while also raising two sons with her husband. Before her debut as an author of original fiction, she wrote fan fiction for ten years and earned herself a readership of over one million.

To find her online, follow her on Facebook, Twitter, Instagram, BookBub and Goodreads. For exclusive content, including outtakes from her books, private giveaways and sneak peeks into her upcoming work, subscribe to her mailing list.

www.facebook.com/KilbyBladesAuthor

www.twitter.com/KilbyBlades

www.instagram.com/KilbyBlades

www.goodreads.com/KilbyBlades

www.bookbub.com/authors/kilby-blades

www.kilbyblades.com/subscribe

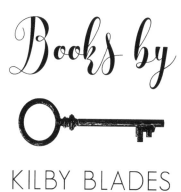

Books by

KILBY BLADES

Novels
Snapdragon (Love Conquers None #1)
Chrysalis (Love Conquers None #2)

Novellas
The Art of Worship

Non-Fiction
Marketing Steamy Romance

82037319R00079

Made in the USA
Columbia, SC
08 December 2017